CHRISTMAS VENDETTA

VALERIE HANSEN

LOVE INSPIRED SUSPENSE
INSPIRATIONAL ROMANCE

LOVE INSPIRED® SUSPENSE
INSPIRATIONAL ROMANCE

ISBN-13: 978-1-335-55470-3

Christmas Vendetta

Copyright © 2021 by Valerie Whisenand

This edition published by arrangement with Harlequin Books S.A.

For questions and comments about the quality of this book, please contact us at CustomerService@Harlequin.com.

Love Inspired
22 Adelaide St. West, 40th Floor
Toronto, Ontario M5H 4E3, Canada
www.LoveInspired.com

Printed in U.S.A.

Be not deceived; God is not mocked:
for whatsoever a man soweth, that shall he also reap.
—*Galatians* 6:7

This book is dedicated to the "givers," the people who use their time and talents for the sake of others, not only in the medical and law enforcement fields but also in ways that silently comfort our hearts and remind us of the unfailing love of God.

ONE

Sandy Lynn Forrester woke abruptly. *Why?* She knuckled her eyelids, wiping away sleep. Had she been having a nightmare? Snow was building outside her bedroom window, piling in ridges where the panes met the sash. The faint scent of pine wafted from the live Christmas tree she and her roommate, Enid, had erected in the living room. Everything seemed normal.

About to relax and drift off again, she heard scraping. A thud. Her breath caught. Throwing aside the blankets, she sat up and swung her feet to the cold floor. The sounds were close yet not inside her room. That left only the living areas or Enid's bedroom. Maybe her friend was sick and needed help.

Sandy Lynn grabbed her robe and finished pulling it on over her fleecy sweatshirt and pants as she reached the short hallway. "Enid? Enid, are you okay?"

The only reply was a muffled cry. *Muffled?* The hair on her arms prickled. *Stop? Turn? Run? No way.* Instinct urged action. Friendship gave it legs.

Padding barefoot to the second bedroom door, she called again. "Hey! Is everything all right in there? I thought I heard you holler."

Nothing. Silence except for her own breathing and the cadence of her rapid heartbeats.

She grasped the doorknob and began to turn it.

Movement jerked it out of her hand but not before momentum had catapulted her into the room. She staggered, got her balance, peered into the dimness and froze. Enid lay doubled up on the floor, eyes squeezed shut, face contorted in pain.

A shadowy figure in a ski mask stepped out from behind the door, one gloved hand brandishing a knife, the other reaching for her.

Sandy Lynn ducked, dodged, tripped and fell, landing close enough to her friend to see the unspoken plea in her wide, glistening eyes. "Enid! What's going on?"

Looming over them both, the shadow cursed. Sandy Lynn's blood iced in her veins and her muscles knotted. *That voice.* It couldn't be Charles Hood. It just couldn't be. He was in prison. Sandy Lynn had gotten their marriage annulled and built a whole new life for herself. Her mind had to be playing tricks on her.

Sandy Lynn watched as the attacker took a tentative step backward, then hesitated. It didn't matter who this man was. He had obviously hurt Enid and would likely do the same to her if she gave him the chance.

There had to be something at hand to use as a defense weapon, but what? The bedside lamp was light and fragile. Slippers on the floor were too soft. The desk chair was too heavy for her to lift and swing. Remembering that Enid had played golf in the summer, Sandy Lynn's gaze darted to the closet. The assailant was blocking her way.

Survival instinct erased all traces of fear. One hand reached for the quilt that had been half-pulled from the bed, and she gave it a mighty yank as she leaped to her feet. It furled between her and the man, obscuring his face, his vision.

He began to swing both arms, batting and slashing at the fabric. Sandy Lynn scrambled toward the closet. She was opening that door when he grabbed a fistful of her robe's collar, also catching hold of her long brown hair.

Pain should have stopped her. Adrenaline overrode it. She twisted and tugged, managing to reach the edge of the golf bag. It crashed to the floor. So did she.

Screaming "No, no, no!" she pulled out a random club and started swinging.

"Hey!" He faltered. Stepped back.

"Get out of here!" Again she swung, this time aiming higher than his ankles, and heard the metal shaft of the club connect with shinbone.

The attacker shouted wordlessly.

Battling the urge to shut her eyes and blot everything out, Sandy Lynn stood and continued defending herself. Again and again the club connected with loud thwacks. He'd dropped his knife and raised both arms to protect his face and head. She knew she was hurting him. How long could she continue before her strength gave out?

Could she last long enough to drive him off, or was he going to eventually pick up his knife and come for her?

Sounds of a scuffle woke Clay Danforth. He stared up at the ceiling and saw the light fixture vibrate. Whatever was happening on the floor above him was violent, which did not bode well for the residents of that apartment.

He listened carefully, seeking confirmation of his initial conclusion. It came in the form of a woman's scream. It didn't matter that he hadn't yet met his neighbors. Somebody up there needed him, and although his authority had ended when he'd left the police force, his concern for fellow citizens had not. He pulled on jeans and boots, palmed his phone long enough to call 911, then slipped a gun into the waistband at the small of his back and headed for the stairway.

Taking the steps two at a time, he rounded the corner and saw a partially open door. Raised voices identified that apartment as the source of the conflict. A woman's screeching demand to be left alone spurred him into a run.

Slamming his shoulder against the outer wall next to the doorjamb, he drew the gun. "Police! Come out with your hands up."

In moments a black-clad figure raced past him and pounded down the stairs. Without knowing any details Clay didn't dare shoot; nor was it prudent to give chase.

Anticipating a second criminal or more, Clay whipped around the corner and took a shooter's stance in the doorway. Something whizzed past his ear and clipped the edge of his shoulder. If he had not been a seasoned veteran, the blow might have caused him to accidentally fire. "Stop! I'm a police officer." Which was sort of still true.

He diverted his aim. His free hand shot out to grab the metal shaft of the club. When he focused on the person holding the leather grip, the effect was mind-blowing. Looking into those familiar hazel eyes, he croaked, "Sandy?"

The impossibility that he would have chosen an apartment directly beneath that of the one woman who had shattered his heart into a thousand pieces was not only astounding—it made him furious with the friend who had talked him into the lease. He would never have listened to Abe and signed the contract if he'd dreamed she lived in the same building. Never in a million years.

Lips parted and trembling, Sandy Lynn pointed to the hallway. "He's getting away!"

Clay snapped back into professional mode. "Was he alone?"

"I think so." She was nodding as the grumbling roar from an accelerating motorcycle broke into the night.

Clay wrested the golf club from her and closed the door behind him with his foot, never relaxing vigilance. "Are you sure?"

"I—I only saw one man." She left him and hurried back to her injured roommate, dropping to her knees. "Enid? Honey, talk to me."

Clay made a cursory search of the tiny apartment, then joined her. "What happened?"

Sandy Lynn's tear-streaked face lifted. "He had a knife. We have to call an ambulance."

"It's done," Clay said. "Move so I can check her over." Because she gave little ground, he shouldered past.

"What are *you* doing here?"

Took her long enough. "Sounds like you're not very glad to see me." He huffed. "Big surprise." While his hands checked Enid's pulse his thoughts raced. Of all the people to encounter after all this time, Sandy Lynn was the absolute worst.

Clay's jaw clenched. The buddy who had told him about the vacant apartment had kept urging him to take advantage of it. If Abe was actually aware of what he'd done, Clay was going to tell him off, and then some.

"Never mind me," Sandy Lynn said with a quaking voice. "Is Enid going to be all right?"

Clay chose to avoid answering as he noticed the

wounded victim's clenched teeth and the barely perceptible shake of her head. She had pulled the corner of a blanket into her arms and was pressing it tightly to her abdomen as the visible edges began to turn crimson.

He redialed the emergency number. "This is Clay Danforth again. There's a seriously wounded victim at the address I gave you for the disturbance. I've secured the immediate scene. Send medics to the second floor. ASAP."

"Affirmative."

"And have responding units keep an eye out for a man on a heavy motorcycle. We think that's how the assailant escaped."

"Copy."

Clay would have suggested that Sandy Lynn put on shoes and go stand in the street to wave down the ambulance if he hadn't been worried about her safety. Just because an attacker had fled didn't mean he wouldn't return.

"Go to your front door and watch for the paramedics," he ordered, trying to keep his voice from reflecting his true concern.

"No. Enid needs me."

The darker-haired young woman on the floor finally spoke. "Do as he says, Sandy."

"But…"

Clay could tell she was undecided so he reinforced the command. "It's the best thing you can do for her right now, okay? Make sure they come to the right place."

"Should I go downstairs then?"

Both Clay and Enid said, "No," and he sensed the effort it took the victim to speak so forcefully. She turned her head aside and coughed, then wiped her lips on the blanket.

He laid a hand of comfort on Enid's shoulder. "Save your strength. Try to slow your pulse. Help should be here in a couple more minutes."

She nodded, then glanced past him toward the doorway and spoke quietly aside. "Look after Sandy, will you?"

"She'll be fine. She's just in shock."

"No." Another cough. "Not now. Later. She needs protection."

"From what?"

Struggling to gather enough breath, Enid whispered, "The guy who did this to me."

Clay saw her eyelids flutter. Her lips were tinged blue. Clay placed his hand over her folded arms to keep pressure on the wound in case she fainted.

Although she winced and gave a little gasp, she continued. "He made a mistake in the dark."

"He thought he was stabbing your roommate?"

Enid nodded once. Then her eyes rolled back in her head and she escaped from the pain.

"In here," Sandy Lynn called, waving both her arms overhead. "Hurry!"

A team of two paramedics, each carrying a red canvas bag, brushed past her into the apartment. She saw Clay speaking to them quietly as they went to work. When he straightened and she glimpsed blood on his hands, she pressed her fingertips to her lips.

Bits and pieces of their last meeting nearly ten years earlier began to gather into coherent thought. He'd said he was enlisting in the air force, so she'd done the only thing she felt she could under those circumstances.

She'd run away from her foster home and married Charles Hood.

Bile tainted her tongue. Fear made her ball her fists and tremble from head to toe. Could the worst mistake of her life have caught up with her? Was it possible Charles had gotten out of prison? The authorities were supposed to notify her if he came up for parole, weren't they?

Yes. Sandy Lynn's nails cut into her palms. But because she trusted no one, she had moved twice without leaving a forwarding address. How hard would the parole board try to locate her? Probably not nearly as hard as her vengeful ex would.

She hurried into the kitchen to grab a roll of paper towels, tearing off several sheets for Clay as she passed. "Here. You can go clean up in the bathroom if you want."

"Okay. Holler at me if they need my help."

"Right." There was little left to Sandy Lynn's imagination as she clutched the roll of paper towels and stared down at her wounded friend. Enid was a nurse. She'd know how badly hurt she was even if she didn't admit it.

"This might be my fault," Sandy Lynn whispered.

A uniformed police officer had entered the apartment. He stopped beyond the carnage and took out a pen and notebook before tapping Sandy Lynn on the shoulder. "Excuse me, ma'am. You think this is your fault? Did you harm that woman?"

"No, no! She's my roommate. Somebody broke in."

"Are you the apartment owner?"

"What? Oh. Yes. Enid and I share the rent."

"What about Danforth, the guy who called this in? Where's he?"

With a shaky breath, she called, "Clay! Living room."

He appeared in seconds, his dark eyes narrow, hair tousled and a towel in his hands. As soon as he spotted the officer he visibly relaxed, continuing to dry his clean hands before offering to shake. "Clay Danforth, detective bureau, downtown Springfield division, recently retired."

The cop shifted his pen to shake hands. "Tucker. I just transferred out of Traffic, but I've heard about you, Detective. Rotten shame."

"Yeah, well… We have other things to worry about tonight."

She saw him tilt his head toward the tableau on the bedroom floor. Enid moaned, bringing tears to Sandy Lynn's eyes. She wanted to go to her dear friend, to kneel beside her on the floor and pray, if nothing else. However, the older of the two medics was using his radio to order a gurney brought up for transport, so she stayed out of the way.

Her fingers were twined so tightly they were whitening. When Clay stepped closer, she wished mightily he'd hold her hands to comfort her the way he used to, but he didn't. Why that oversight hurt after all this time was a question she set aside for later.

The police officer stuck with them. "What can you tell me about this assailant? Did either of you get a good look at him?"

"I think I did," Sandy Lynn said while Clay shook his head.

"Would you be able to pick him out of a lineup?"

"Not by sight. He was wearing a mask." She licked her parched lips. "I thought I recognized his voice, though. Only that's impossible. That man's in prison."

"His name?" The officer was writing as she spoke.

"Charles Hood." There was nothing sinister about

a name, yet merely mentioning it took her back to his cruelty and his eventual sentencing. What he had done was unspeakable. The only good part about his abuse was that it had convinced her to flee and have their marriage annulled.

Clay was frowning. "You're sure he's not out on parole?"

"He's not supposed to be eligible for a couple more years." Fighting back tears, she watched the paramedics lift Enid onto the gurney and wheel her out the door while a third man held up an IV bag and kept pace with them.

"Okay," Clay said. He turned to Tucker. "Let's get the questioning over with so she can get dressed and I can drive her to the hospital."

Sandy Lynn resisted. "No. I have to ride with Enid. She'll need me there when she wakes up."

Tucker held out an arm to block her exit. "Not so fast, ma'am. You have more explaining to do first."

"But…"

Clay cleared his throat as if his words were sticking there. "I'll vouch for her, stay with her and deliver her to your station once her friend is stable."

Just because they had a history didn't mean she was willing to bow to his wishes now. "No way. If they won't let me go along in the ambulance, I'll drive myself."

"I won't be responsible for you behind the wheel when you've had a shock like this," Clay said flatly.

"Who asked you to be?" The rancor in her tone surprised her enough to make her slightly ashamed. Blushing and fighting more tears, she looked away.

"We can take your car, assuming you have one," Clay said, "but I'm driving it."

Sandy Lynn glanced at the police officer, hoping

for moral support. All she read in his expression was agreement with Clay.

"Men." She sniffled. "All right. I'll let you drive me, but only because I'm shaking so much inside. Don't think you can go back to ordering me around the way you used to."

"What? I never…" He broke off, clearly upset. "Give me your keys and at least go get some shoes on. I'll warm up the car. Tucker can escort you out when you're ready."

The officer nodded as if taking orders from a civilian was normal procedure. That told her how much other cops admired Clay, even though he was no longer one of them. She paused to take a ring of keys from the kitchen counter and toss them to him. "It's the blue car in my space. You can't miss it."

Wheeling, wordless, he was gone.

In minutes she had donned jeans, slipped her feet into lined boots, grabbed a warm jacket and was back, passing Tucker. "Let's go."

"I can't leave the scene," he said. "Have to wait for crime scene techs. They'll be here in a sec."

That didn't slow Sandy Lynn a bit. She jerked open the door to the hallway. "Don't you have a partner?"

"Out sick. We were shorthanded tonight."

"Too bad," she called back. "I'm leaving."

It wasn't until she was halfway down the stairs that she noticed how dark the passageway was. Most of the overhead lights that usually illuminated the stairs were out.

Shivering, she did her best to stay steady as she began to hurry even more, sliding one hand down the banister. Something felt damp and tacky in spots. She recoiled and slowed for balance and stability while she stared at her upturned hand.

Reality bit like a swarm of angry bees. Enid's attacker had apparently left bloody fingerprints behind, and by touching the banister she had probably smudged or erased them.

"My fault," Sandy Lynn muttered, continuing to the first floor. "All my fault. Especially if Charles did this."

That thought alone was enough to weaken her knees and make her wish she'd had the presence of mind to grab another golf club on her way out. Time away from his constant threats had apparently dimmed her sense of self-preservation.

She clamped her jaw. After tonight, her defenses needed to be fortified. Remembrance of Charles Hood comingled with memories of Clay and caused her to add, "*All* of my defenses."

TWO

Condensation of his exhaled breaths proved how cold the night was. Clay hardly noticed. His focus was on what he'd just learned. It seemed impossible that he and Sandy Lynn actually resided in the same building, or that a good friend like Abe had known what he was doing when he'd kept insisting that this was the perfect apartment to lower living costs while Clay looked for a new job. What a cruel joke. The whole Christmas season was emotionally fraught under normal circumstances. Adding a lost love and a ruined career to the mix was going to make this season Clay's worst ever.

He had ducked into his own apartment for a jacket and boots before proceeding to the car. His motorcycle, covered with a tarp, stood nearby in its own spot. He'd position the car in the best spot to watch for Sandy. "Sandy Lynn," he corrected himself. She'd always been a stickler for the Southern version of her first name. More fool him for not checking the mailboxes to see if he recognized any of his new neighbors.

No wonder he was distracted, considering all the other things on his mind lately, he reasoned, satisfied with that excuse. Even if he was eventually able to prove himself innocent of evidence mishandling, his law enforcement days were over. Suspicion would follow him wherever he went, staining his record before he even started. As long as some shady lawyer didn't convince a judge to freeze his bank accounts he'd be all right for a while. After his savings ran out, who knew?

Condensation had formed on the insides of the windows before Clay found the car's defrost control. He let the motor warm up for a few short minutes, then backed out from under the carport and drove to the rear exit. Exhaust from the idling engine billowed, its cloud obscuring the area behind the car.

Clumps of snowflakes had already begun to accumulate on the front and rear windows. This was a wet, nasty snowfall, the kind that made riding his motorcycle feel like sloshing through icy streams. It was also treacherous, especially if other drivers didn't see him, or underestimated their speed and braking time on slick streets.

A single light mounted on the rear of the apartment building cast a faint yellow halo, which was another reason Clay had chosen to wait close by. Leaning over to watch through the passenger-side window, he wasn't surprised to see Sandy Lynn come out. Unfortunately, she was alone. So much for a police escort.

He was circling the car to open her door when he saw her stop dead in her tracks. She stared into the exhaust cloud. Her lips parted. Raising both hands in front of her, she started to back away.

She didn't scream. She didn't have to. One look told him all he needed to know. Clay had his gun in hand before he finished rounding the car. He didn't know what she'd seen and he didn't care. It was enough to know it had frightened her.

"Where? What?" he yelled.

She pointed.

"I don't see anything."

"He was right there."

Keeping his thumb on the gun's safety, he pointed it in the general direction she'd indicated. "Get in the car and lock the doors."

Although Sandy Lynn did open the car door she froze again, so he grasped her upper arm and gave her a shove. "I said, get in."

Resistance crumbled. She opened her mouth as if she intended to argue, and then she slid into the seat.

Clay slammed the door. "Lock it. Now."

The locks clicked. He steeled himself for possible attack, took a deep breath, crouched and started into the exhaust cloud.

To reach the master control for the door locks, Sandy Lynn had had to slide across to the driver's seat. Secure inside her car, she decided to stay where she was and watch Clay. It was quickly apparent how impossible that was with all the condensation, so she switched off the engine.

Counting to herself, *One Mississippi, two Mississippi, three Mississippi*, she continued to peer into the side mirror. Snow obscured some of her view, but the rest of the picture was slowly clearing. Now she could make out one person, creeping along bent over and moving away from her car. That was Clay, or at least she hoped it was. Beyond him, swirling snow and mist was masking the scene while her closed windows gathered more moisture.

She made a fist and used it to clear the inside of one pane, searching for the large figure she'd seen when she'd first stepped outside. There was nothing there other than Clay, and even his image was beginning to fade into the storm.

"Should I open the door to look?" she asked herself, knowing the answer was a big fat *no*. Instead of accepting a logical conclusion, she decided to seek divine input and prayed, "Please, Father? I'm worried about him. Will you be with me if I open the door to see better?"

Her left hand hovered over the interior handle for long moments before she curled her icy fingers around it. *Squeeze? Don't squeeze?* Oh, how she hated indecision. "Father?"

No clear answer came to her. At least not the one she wanted. That was the problem, wasn't it? She'd spent the first seventeen years of her life taking orders of one kind or another, some delivered sanely but most shouted and backed up by physical violence. That was what had made her vow to become her own woman, to choose a path without listening to advice and to always stand up for herself.

Running into Clay Danforth so unexpectedly had apparently rocketed her emotions ten years into the past and had resulted in her current lack of initiative, she reasoned. That would never do.

Sandy Lynn closed her hand on the door handle. Heard the click as it unlatched. Still, she didn't start to push the door open until she had rechecked the mirrors.

Snow was still falling, but the flakes had now separated enough that they weren't clumping, meaning it was getting colder out there. She shivered, pausing to fasten the snap at the neck of her quilted coat and lift the hood to cover her hair.

That delay was enough to change everything.

A contorted, ski-masked face loomed out of the dimness, its mouth a gaping leer.

Sandy Lynn pulled in enough air to scream and managed a shrill squeak.

Two splayed hands smashed against the car door, slamming it closed with a bang.

She fell back, stunned, trembling, barely able to breathe. As her back arched over the padded center console and her ribs glanced off the steering wheel, her feet left the floor. Knees bent, she raised both boots to aim a kick, assuming the masked assailant intended to come after her.

Why, oh why had she unlocked that door? She felt foolish as well as penitent. The notion that she was too stubborn for her own good came and went, followed by the realization that she had been protected inside the car until she had thwarted Clay's plans. *And God's?* she asked herself. The idea that her heavenly Father might have brought that impossible man back into her life at the precise moment when she most needed him was hard to swallow.

However, so was dying.

Time seemed to slow. Action outside the window took on a surreal effect.

The eyes and mouth of the black ski mask disappeared as its wearer spun around.

There was a clear shout of "Freeze!"

Sandy Lynn curled into a fetal position on the seat, her arms clamping around her head, the hood scrunching forward. Men were fighting out there, and repeated collisions with the side of the car made it rock. Even through covered ears she could make out two different masculine voices.

Someone fired a gun! She didn't hear or feel a bullet hit the car, so it was possible the shooter had aimed away. Was Clay the target?

Pain squeezed her chest as if her heart was cracking. She was able to deny that sensation by substituting another possible conclusion—that the shot had merely been a warning.

She'd built a figurative stone wall around herself and so far it was holding. Barely. There had been a time when she would have been honored and delighted to have Clay stand firm in her defense. As a matter of fact, he had. More than once. But now, after all that had transpired to break them up and break her heart in the process, he was the last person she wanted to accept as her champion.

All noise outside the car ceased. Sandy Lynn strained to listen, but nothing came through past her pounding pulse beats and ragged breathing.

Slowly, deliberately, she raised herself to a sitting position. Condensation again coated the window she had cleared. The car door remained firmly closed but, she realized with a start, it was still unlocked.

"If I can't see out, nobody can see in," she assured herself, wondering if that was true. Not that it mattered, since the guy in the ski mask already knew where she was. If he remained out there, she needed to relock the car.

"But suppose Clay needs help?" she added. A lump of concern blocked her throat, and tears clouded her vision. If he was okay he'd come back to the car, wouldn't he? And he hadn't done so. Therefore, the logical conclusion was that he could not.

So, what did she have handy for a defense weapon this time? Enid had bought her a can of pepper spray a long time ago and she had tossed it into the glove compartment. If it was still there...

Papers, manuals, the car's registration, packets of condiments and various fast-food napkins hit the floor as she pawed through the detritus. There!

It was impossible to read the faint expiration date on the bottom of the small canister, but having it in hand was enough to provide the courage she needed to open a door once more. This time she exited on the passenger side.

Listening and scanning the snowy night, she thought she heard a moan. With one finger on the spray nozzle she crept around the car. The single yellow circle of light from the apartment building illuminated the snow. A figure was slowly rising from the ground. He held a gun.

Sandy Lynn aimed the spray directly at his head. If he did or said one tiny thing wrong, she was going to let him have it.

Instead, he put a hand to his head and leaned against her car.

"Clay?"

Instead of answering, he started to turn.

Reflexes tightened her grip on the canister. She stifled a scream.

The man's free hand shot out and grabbed her wrist just as a weak stream of pepper spray sputtered out ineffectively.

That freed her voice and she shrieked, loud and high.

"It's me," he shouted over her scream. "Stop trying to blind me."

"I thought..."

"Yeah, I hoped you weren't trying to spray *me*," he said roughly. "Let go of that thing."

"It was all I had," Sandy Lynn protested. If he had not been grasping her wrist, she didn't think she could have kept from falling back onto the car for balance.

"I told you to stay locked in. What part of that didn't you understand?"

"I know what you said. But I heard a shot."

"And you were coming to the rescue?" He huffed. "That doesn't say much for your confidence in me."

His off-putting attitude was helping her recover. "You're bulletproof? What a helpful skill."

The canister left her grip as he wrested it away and stepped back. She could see he was upset and wanted to tell him that she'd only tried to help because he still meant something to her, but she figured that was the last thing she should admit. Having him around again was bad enough without complicating matters by dredging up the past.

"I shot into the ground when he tried to escape," Clay informed her. "Nobody was in danger."

"Right." By this time she was stable enough to fist her hands on her hips, certain he could see her by the yellow light. "So you decided to lie down in the snow and rest while you waited to see if he'd surrender?"

"I slipped, that's all." He shoved the gun into his waistband and opened the car door. "Get in." When she stood firm, he added, "Do you want to go see Enid, or not?"

"Of course I do."

He closed her door as soon as she was safely seated and got behind the wheel.

"Are you sure you're fit to drive?" she asked, thinking of his head. "How hard did he hit you?"

"I told you. I slipped on the melting snow."

"If you say so."

"I do."

The sight of Clay's strong, capable hands on the wheel and the firm set of his jaw stopped her from nagging. She might be holding a grudge about the way he'd abandoned her in the past, but she didn't doubt his innate capabilities. Nor was she worried that he would purposely put anyone in jeopardy.

If she got the chance, she intended to ask about the ending of his career in law enforcement. The cop at her apartment had intimated that Clay's dismissal had been unfair, and that was all she'd managed to glean. Considering her concern for her dear friend Enid, Sandy Lynn was surprised she'd retained even a tidbit about Clay.

And yet, she had. That was probably not a good sign. Not good at all. Especially since she was going to have to get away from him ASAP, before the best of her memories softened her heart so much he could break it again.

THREE

Stalling for time, Clay parked in front of the hospital instead of by the emergency entrance.

"I said, drive around the back."

"I heard you. This is better."

"Oh, for the love of…"

"I'm not trying to keep you from being with Enid. I'm thinking of her. The less distraction the hospital staff has, the better they'll be able to do their jobs."

The look in Sandy Lynn's eyes when she turned to him again was devoid of her earlier ire. When she asked, "How bad was it?" he wondered if giving his opinion was wise.

He cleared his throat. "Um, bad. It looked like she'd lost a lot of blood. Starting the IV and transporting was critical."

A slow nod of Sandy Lynn's head showed that she understood much of what he was not putting into words.

Clay climbed out and met her at the passenger door. Starting to take her arm, he decided there was no need. If she showed signs of being faint he'd be close enough to reach out and catch her. Truth to tell, she was recovering better than most of the victims he'd encountered as a cop. Her problem was the opposite. Instead of becoming hysterical in the face of tragedy, she went too far the other way. Right now, she looked basically shut down, emotionless. That wasn't good, either.

He fell into step beside her. "Remember, even if your friend is unconscious she may be able to hear us talking so don't discuss her condition. And whatever you do, don't start weeping and wailing. It's bad for the patient's morale."

Sandy Lynn's head snapped around. Her eyes were slightly puffy but narrowed in a scowl, and her jaw was set. "Do I look like I'm about to lose it?"

Chancing the hint of a smile, Clay nodded. "Well, you do have a good set of lungs on you. That scream when you were trying to pepper spray me was a lulu."

"If the spray had worked you wouldn't be laughing."

"Fight or flight," he said. "It's instinctive. Most folks will run if they can. Really exceptional people will stand their ground. Those are rare."

"Are you giving me a compliment?"

"For getting out of the car armed with an outdated weapon? Not hardly."

"Oh. Well, thanks anyway. I learned the hard way to fight back." Although her pace toward the hospital was rapid, he heard her add, "That was the only good thing about my marriage." She gave a wry chuckle, "Except for the end of it."

"I wouldn't wish a bad marriage on anyone regardless of any lessons you think you learned from the experience."

"You're right about that. The only thing I did wrong was jump into a situation I should have been savvy enough to avoid. Once I was in it, having the courage to admit my mistake and get out was what saved me."

"Standing up for yourself, you mean."

"Yes." She smiled. "Inner strength and conviction come in handy when dealing with the seven- and eight-year-olds I teach, too. They can get pretty rowdy." Her smile widened.

"So that's the career you chose." He wasn't surprised. Sandy Lynn had always acted motherly toward her foster siblings when he'd lived next door to the group home.

"Yes. Eventually. I had to settle down and work hard, but I made it. I'm surprised you hadn't heard."

"I was working up in Kansas City until a few months ago when I decided to come home." He made a face of disgust. "Not the best career choice, as it turned out."

"Sorry."

"Yeah. Me, too."

He wanted to tell her he was proud of her accomplishments. He didn't yield to the urge. The years of their fractured friendship were not something he wanted to explore, let alone repair. Her career was solid while his was on the skids, not to mention the possibility he might be wrongly convicted if his enemies managed to convince a judge to indict. Sandy Lynn had pulled herself out of poverty through hard work and courage. Yes, she'd made the mistake of marrying an abusive man, but she still wasn't out of the woods.

As Clay saw it, all he had to do was stick by her until her assailant was caught. After that he could walk away. The second element would be harder, no matter how difficult the first was.

Plus, he had to make sure his ruined reputation did no harm to hers. If ever there was a good reason to keep his emotional distance, that was it.

By the time they had circled the small hospital and entered the doors to the ER, Sandy Lynn was fully in control. She breezed past the reception desk and straight-armed the swinging door to the emergency treatment area. "Enid?"

Following close behind, Clay touched her arm and she jumped, whirling on him. "What?"

"Calm down. We'll find her if she's still here."

"Why wouldn't she be?"

"They may have taken her to surgery," Clay said quietly. "Let's ask before you go berserk and start tearing down curtains."

"I never go berserk," Sandy Lynn replied stiffly.

With a cynical chuckle he gestured at her. "What do you call *this*?"

"Strong concern. Anybody'd be worried."

"I'll give you that," Clay said. "I see someone I know. Come on."

A petite, dark-haired nurse broke into a wide grin when he greeted her. "Hey, Phoebe. I wonder if you can help us."

The brief look the nurse gave Sandy Lynn was clearly not friendly. "I heard you were back in town, Clay. It took you long enough to come see me."

"I've been busy moving into a smaller apartment," he said. "We'll have to get together sometime. Right now, I—we need your help."

"That's what I'm here for." A wry chuckle. "Does your friend there have a problem?"

Sandy Lynn sensed an underlying hint of jealousy but she chose the high road and smiled. "No problem. I'm Sandy Lynn Forrester. Clay and I were buddies when we were kids. My roommate was brought in tonight, and I came to check on her."

"Name?" Phoebe asked.

"Enid Bloom."

"Enid! Why didn't you say so in the first place? She's been taken up to the OR."

"You know her?" Clay asked.

"Well enough, considering how big this hospital staff is. She's a great nurse. Everybody likes her."

"Okay. Where should we go to find out how she's doing?"

"Waiting room. Third floor rear," the nurse said, her words clipped. "I heard the guy with the knife said he got the wrong woman. Is that true?"

"Not the best timing," Clay told her, scowling.

Sandy Lynn wasn't about to let it drop. "What do you mean, the wrong woman?"

"Just what I said. Enid was conscious by the time the ambulance boys brought her in, and she told us what happened."

Sandy Lynn's eyes narrowed and she turned on Clay. "You already knew. *That's* why you insisted on coming with me."

"I did. But you were in no shape to be behind the wheel of a car, either. You're still not."

Furious, she was headed toward a bank of elevators before he finished speaking. When he did catch up she was ready. "You're the one with police connections, so find out where Charles is and why I thought the voice was so familiar."

"I intend to."

"Good." She kept her gaze fixed on the elevator doors, too upset to think clearly, let alone find the right words to scold him. That lack was not a good sign. Not good at all. Losing her cool tended to cause her to make snap decisions, and history had proven how poor those could be.

She blew a sigh, disgusted with herself, and concentrated on the problem at hand. Enid's welfare came first, of course. Then, she'd need to find them both another place to live, particularly if the attacker had been Charles. Even if it was a stranger, he might return, so the smartest move was to leave that apartment and go elsewhere. Third, there was the advantage of getting away from Clay Danforth. As long as they were renting in the same building, he was far too close by. Too handy. Too likely to drop into her life at odd moments the way he had tonight.

He may have saved my life, Sandy Lynn told herself as the elevator doors whooshed open. *May* have? She huffed. There was little question that his arrival had turned the tide in her favor. The same went for his defending her at the car outside the apartment building.

She shut her eyes. Clenched her teeth and her fists. Fought off the sensation of being looked after. Being safe. It wasn't as all-encompassing as the peace and comfort she drew from her restored faith in God, but it was nice enough to make her blush.

Two nurses were waiting for the elevator when it stopped on the third floor. Clay politely stood back to let all the women pass, then got off. Sandy Lynn didn't have to look back to know exactly where he was. She could sense his presence as if they were nearly as in tune as they had been years before.

Concern for Enid made her wish for Clay's physical comfort—the touch of his hand on hers, the support of his arm around her shoulders. Concern for herself negated that wish and others like it. She had her reasons, good ones, and wasn't about to revive a romance that couldn't go anywhere. There was no need to reveal the end result of the damage Charles had done to her during that final beating. It was enough that she knew she could never bear children. Her students helped fill the void for the present, and she wasn't ready to think beyond her teaching years. One thing she had vowed to never do was consider marriage again. Ever.

Hiding another unwelcome flush of her cheeks by turning away, Sandy Lynn led the way to the nurses station, inquired about Enid and was directed to the surgical waiting room. It was sparsely decorated for Christmas, with a garland of holly and berries atop the line of windows and twinkling white lights outlining them as well as the two entry doors, one at each end. Dog-eared magazines lay scattered on a coffee table, and a pristine Bible waited on an end table in a corner.

An older woman, knitting, was the only other person present, and by choosing the single chair between her and the end of the row Sandy was able to keep Clay at bay. Although he didn't look happy about her choice, he positioned himself across from them and watched the doors. That degree of diligence made her shiver.

"I'm sure we're perfectly safe here," Clay told her. "Nobody in his right mind would consider causing more trouble in such a public place."

Sandy Lynn huffed. "That's the problem, isn't it? If Charles is the one doing all this, he may not be in his right mind."

Their elderly companion inhaled sharply. "Sorry. I don't mean to eavesdrop, but is there some reason to be afraid?"

Clay said, "There's nothing for you to worry about, ma'am," wishing he fully believed it. He slipped off his jacket, then palmed his cell phone to check text messages. The final one was enough to raise his eyebrows. "Uh-oh."

Sandy Lynn leaned forward. "What? Tell me."

"It's not a parole situation the way you thought. Hood was in a group working on highway cleanup. There was an accident nearby and, in the confusion, several of the inmates escaped."

"It *was* him!"

"They say not, but it's not a maximum security prison so the situation is worth rechecking."

"Do you really believe he's still locked up, or are you trying to influence me again? Don't you think it's better for me to be on my guard rather than feel too complacent?"

Clay nodded, hoping his aura of calm would rub off on her. Before he had a chance to answer, their elderly companion stuffed her knitting into a tote, got to her feet and prepared to leave. "Unless you two tell me what's going on, I'm leaving. I don't care if my poor husband is in surgery. I'm not going to sit here without knowing."

"It's simple," Clay explained, slowly and quietly. "There was an altercation at Ms. Forrester's apartment. Her roommate was injured and is currently being treated." He got to his feet and flashed a card in his wallet, hoping the concerned woman didn't insist on looking too closely and discover it was for a gym membership, not law enforcement. "Clay Danforth. Springfield Police."

"Oh, gracious. This is disturbing. I'm sorry. I simply can't stay here." Halfway to the door, she glanced back and said, "I hope your friend makes it."

"And you thought I was being irrational," Sandy Lynn remarked when the woman was gone. "Not hanging around to see if her husband's surgery went well? That's…weird."

"Yeah." Clay's brow wrinkled. Something about the woman's behavior was off. Not much, mind you, but just enough to raise the hairs on the nape of his neck.

Standing, he studied the doorway, watching, waiting, thinking. "Stay here for a few minutes while I go see where she went."

"Why?"

"There was something strange about the way that she was acting."

"You scared her by talking about the attack, that's all."

"I'm not going far. I won't leave you. I promise."

"I never said I needed company," she countered. "Go. Do your thing, whatever it is. Now that I know I was imagining Charles' voice and he isn't on the loose I won't worry as much."

"You still need to be vigilant in case he sent one of his fellow inmates in his place."

"That's possible since he's a pathological liar," Sandy Lynn said. "He may have convinced some innocent party to help him."

Highly likely, Clay thought. Allegiances formed in prison tended to be strong, especially if accompanied by a cash payment.

"True," Clay admitted, glancing at the wall clock, "Give me five minutes to check with hospital security. I'll hurry back."

"Take your time. I'm fine."

What he wanted to say was, *Yes, but for how long?* Which he wisely kept to himself. After checking the hallway in both directions, he walked quickly to the nearest nurses station. It wasn't staffed, so he grabbed a phone off a desk and pushed the button labeled Security.

A laconic voice answered. "Yeah?"

"Security?"

"That's us. What's up? Is Margie having a fit again?"

"I don't know what you're talking about. I want to report a possible threat on the third floor, surgery west. Can you send up a man so I can brief him?"

"Who is this?" The voice had taken on a harsh tone.

"Clay Danforth, Springfield Police."

"Danforth? What kind of joke is this? My brother-in-law's on the force, and I know you ain't a cop no more."

"Never mind that. A stabbing victim is in surgery right now, and her roommate needs additional protection until I can get a regular officer up here."

"Okay, okay, but this better be on the up-and-up. I'll radio the man stationed on three and have him meet you in the waiting room. Will that do?"

"Fine."

Just as Clay was hanging up the receiver, he saw movement out of the corner of his eye. The older woman from the waiting room was speaking to a much larger man dressed in dark clothing. Because the two were standing close together and seemed to be speaking privately, his nerves tingled.

The woman pointed back down the hall to the nearby waiting room where Clay had left Sandy Lynn and nodded.

The man whirled and Clay saw that a ski mask covered his face. That wasn't unusual garb in the winter, but it was odd to have kept it on after coming inside.

Moving rapidly, the darkly clad figure caught the doorjamb of the small room in one gloved hand and swung through.

Moments later, already on his way back to Sandy Lynn at a run, Clay heard her start to scream.

FOUR

Sandy Lynn backed into a side chair before maneuvering to put it between herself and the man in black. Subconsciously sizing him up and looking for characteristics that would prove he was her abusive ex, she grew puzzled. This guy was dressed like the knife wielder in her apartment, yet something told her he wasn't the same person.

One loud scream was all she permitted herself before stiffening her spine and facing him boldly. "Who are you?"

She watched his mouth start to open as if to answer, but he never got the chance. The sound of boots pounding across the hard floor was followed by a blur of action as Clay Danforth rocketed into the waiting room and tackled the masked man. They both went down. Hard.

Sandy Lynn expected Clay to pull his gun, and then she remembered that he'd left it out in her car because he was no longer an official member of the police force and firearms were prohibited inside the hospital. She started to lift the side chair, realized it was unwieldy and, instead, circled the struggling men. If Clay started to lose the fight she'd have to step in to help him, of course.

Somehow. Hopefully, he'd triumph and she could stay out of it. Battling with fists reminded her too strongly of her unhappy childhood, and she avoided physical confrontations as much as possible.

Clay was a formidable opponent, skilled and quick, but the other man was larger, heavier, which gave him a slight advantage.

Braced to assist her old friend despite their estrangement, she hesitated for seconds that seemed more like hours. Causing pain to another human being was inexcusable, yet the more the men grappled, rolling over and over, the more it looked as if she was going to be forced to step in. Still, she waited, hoping and praying for Clay's victory.

The other man landed a punch on Clay's jaw and his head jerked back. Sandy Lynn took a step forward. Clay's back was on the floor. The attacker raised his arm again, preparing to deliver another stunning blow.

"No!" Sandy Lynn leaped forward and grabbed him by the forearm. He threw her aside with a muttered curse.

She recovered, glad she was still wearing her padded jacket. Clay was faltering and about to receive a thorough beating. That, she could not allow. By this time the adrenaline surging through her system provided enough added strength to easily heft the chair and raise it in front of her, legs pointing out.

Someone moved quickly into her peripheral vision. It was the elderly woman. "Go get help!" Sandy Lynn shouted. "Hurry."

Instead, the woman reached into her tote bag and pulled out a long metal knitting needle.

"Don't hurt my friend," Sandy Lynn shouted. "He's helping us."

The attacker cocked his arm to swing.

Sandy Lynn's jaw dropped when she saw the old woman slap the knitting needle into his upraised hand and heard her yell, "Get him, boy. Finish him."

Nothing made sense. Watching this scene unfold was like entering a theater in the middle of an action movie and getting all the characters mixed up.

Only one thing was clear. Clay was about to be stabbed. That was more than enough to spur her to action.

Once she started the chair swinging in an arc, she couldn't have stopped its forward path if she'd wanted to. And she certainly didn't want to.

The leading leg hit the masked man in the forehead, glanced off his ski mask and shoved the old woman out of the way, while the second and third chair legs connected with the thug's upraised arm and knocked the knitting needle out of his hand.

He howled and jumped away.

Momentum carried Sandy Lynn around in a full circle and brought her back to the starting point while gravity pulled the chair closer and closer to the floor. She staggered, trying to brace herself, and used all her strength to keep it from colliding with Clay's prone body.

The masked man and old woman broke away and made for the door. Were they really working together? Was it even possible that someone had found her this quickly after the initial attack at her apartment?

When the man in black hesitated long enough to give the woman a hand, Sandy Lynn was certain they were a team. A deadly alliance that was bent on harming her.

Falling to her knees beside Clay, she helped him rise and face the vacant doorway. Their assailants were gone.

He shook his head to clear it, investigating his jaw with his fingertips before asking, "Was that who I thought it was?"

"Our little old lady? Yes. But the man in the mask wasn't Charles."

Clay was raking back his hair with his fingers. "Are you sure?"

"Positive," Sandy Lynn said, sorry that there was a tinge of disappointment in her voice. "This guy was too big. Too heavy."

"He could have put on weight in prison."

"Yes, but he couldn't grow six inches taller. That wasn't my ex."

"Okay."

Clay had his phone out and was starting to place a call when an injured security guard lurched through the doorway and pointed a gun at him. "Hands up, mister. And lose the weapon."

Seeing him holding his head and sensing how primed the guard was to shoot, Sandy Lynn stepped between him and Clay with both hands raised, palms facing out. "It's all over, Officer. The bad guys ran off. This man is okay. And that's not a weapon. It's just his phone."

Although it took the guard longer than she would have liked to accept her statement and lower his aim, she knew the immediate threat had passed. It was a relief to see curious hospital personnel gathering in the hallway. That would help if she needed witnesses.

Clay remained beside her, hands also up, the cell phone held between thumb and forefinger. "Call the local police if you doubt which side I'm on," he told the guard.

The meaningful look Sandy Lynn gave the nervous guard was meant to confirm Clay's words. Unfortunately, his reaction was not positive. He waved his pistol. "Over there, both of you, while I sort this out."

Sandy Lynn led the way, looking up at Clay as she eased into a chair. His left eye was starting to turn purple and there was a deep scowl on his face.

She was about to commiserate when he leaned closer and asked, "What next, huh?"

"Hey, don't look at me. I'm just here because my best friend is in surgery. You didn't have to come along."

"Yes, I did," Clay replied with a stern look. "And you know it."

The headache Clay was nursing made him testy. Facing the police, as well as hospital security, and trying to explain what had occurred wasn't helping, either. What he wanted to do was haul Sandy Lynn off and find a good place to hide her. Someplace safe and secure, yet accessible to him in case she needed more protection. The idea that her nemesis had been her ex had been comforting in that it gave them a specific culprit to pursue—until she'd countered with a different ID. If their problem wasn't Charles Hood, then who was it? And how was he going to figure out what was really going on without first learning the identity of the second man in a ski mask?

Time passed as quickly as could be expected, given the circumstances. He kept a close eye on Sandy Lynn during the police questioning, until a couple of his former fellow officers had shown up and started interfering by drawing her away. The only reason he put up with that was for Sandy Lynn's sake. She needed the entire force on her side if she hoped to survive these repeated attacks. The last thing he wanted was to have guilt by association with him undermine her reputation.

The arrival of his friend, Sergeant Matthews, sent a wave of relief through Clay. He greeted him surreptitiously in order to keep the other cops from taking special notice. "Abe. Out of uniform? What brings you here?"

"When I heard the call on my scanner and recognized your new address, I figured this is where you'd probably end up."

Clay scowled. "You and I need to have a long, serious talk about my new home. Did you know who lived upstairs when you were pushing me to choose that apartment building?"

"Me? Naw. Who lives upstairs?"

The denial might have sounded more genuine if Abe had not been gazing across the room at Sandy Lynn and smiling.

Clay huffed. "As if you didn't know." He shook his head in disgust. "I thought you were my friend."

"I am." Abe's grin spread and his eyes twinkled, reflecting the Christmas lights strung around the room. "Just trying to help out a buddy."

"Yeah? Well stop it, okay? I have enough problems already."

"There's no way anybody's going to be able to prove you stole drugs from the locked evidence room, because you didn't do it."

"From your lips to the chief's ears," Clay said. "You and I both know I'm innocent, but there's more than one guy at our station who's sure I'm dirty." His sober sidelong glance at two other officers in the room pointed them out without naming names.

"Yeah, I know," Abe replied. "But they won't fool the chief. He's already questioning the evidence they supposedly found in your car."

"It was enough to get me suspended. He might as well have fired me at that point, because suspicion was all it took to cost me most of my friends."

Abe patted him on the upper arm. "Not me, buddy. I'm on your side all the way."

"Just don't get yourself canned for defending me," Clay warned. "I need at least one loyal inside man. Which reminds me. Double-check the info you texted me about Charles Hood, will you? If he's still incarcerated, like they told you the first time you asked, try to make sure there hasn't been a mix-up."

Abe snorted derisively. "Are you kidding me? They'd better know who's in and who's missing, or you won't be the only one looking for a new job."

Sobering, Clay nodded. "I'm hoping they're wrong and Hood put one over on them."

"Why?"

"Because, if he isn't behind the repeated attacks on Sandy Lynn, she's got a brand-new enemy and no clue as to who wants to hurt her."

"But she's okay, right?"

"For now." Clay raked his fingers through his hair to comb it back. "Unfortunately, her roommate has been insisting that she was knifed by somebody who was after Sandy Lynn and after what just happened here I'm convinced she was right."

"What did happen, exactly?"

"Another attempt to harm her," Clay said, looking toward the small group across the room and settling his gaze on the pretty teacher. "Any doubts I had that Enid was collateral damage are gone. Sandy Lynn was supposed to be the victim."

There was no way she was going to acknowledge Clay's obvious interest or meet his stare. Yes, he had defended her for the third time in one night, but that didn't give him back his special place in her heart. He'd had his chance years ago and had blown it. She was a different person now. A woman who took care of herself and made her own decisions.

She approached one of the police officers who had been questioning her. "Excuse me. Are we finished? I'd like to go find out how my friend Enid is doing."

"You can go as soon as the techs take your prints and a DNA swab. Just don't leave town."

Because he had given her a snide smile as he issued the warning, Sandy Lynn wasn't sure he was serious. "Really? Why not?"

"We're not through investigating the incident at your apartment."

He elbowed his partner, a smaller cop who was also looking too smug. "Besides, since you've started keeping company with a druggie, you have to expect some suspicion to stick to you."

"What are you talking about?"

Both men began to grin at her as if she was simple-minded. The second one gestured toward Clay. "He didn't tell you? He stole a bunch of meth from our evidence room. Maybe other drugs, too."

That statement was so ridiculous it arched Sandy's eyebrows. "Oh, come on. Clay Danforth? No way."

The first cop shrugged. "Evidence says otherwise. You'd be smart to ditch him. I would if I was you."

"Well, you're *not* me," Sandy Lynn countered. "I practically grew up with that man, and he's as honest as they come."

Rather than add more personal information, she spun on her heel and strode away. In the confines of the crowded waiting room there were few choices of where to stand, so she chose the most distant from the unfriendly officers and joined Clay. A nod was her greeting.

When the lanky, dark-haired officer with Clay smiled at her she felt a twinge of memory. "Do I know you?"

Clay looked amused. "You don't remember Abe?"

"Abe? Sorry. No."

Both men laughed, which made Sandy Lynn curious enough to dive deeper into memories. "Hold on. Your first name is Mike. Mikey! I'm sure it is. You used to visit Clay when he lived next door to my last foster home."

"Right. I was a lot shorter then. And pudgy. After I got so tall and thin, folks started comparing me to Abe Lincoln and the nickname stuck." He rolled his eyes. "Some of my old friends refuse to call me anything else."

"That's mean."

"Could be worse. How have you been, Sandy Lynn? I heard you were teaching in the elementary school."

"Yes." How much more he might know bothered her. "Has Clay filled you in on my checkered past?"

"Only that your ex isn't somebody you want to see again."

"That's putting it mildly. Is there some way you can check with the prison and make sure he's still there?"

"I already have," Abe told her, sobering, "but I'll be

glad to ask for regular updates. Last I heard, Charles Hood was still in residence."

"Did you look at his record?" she asked.

"Briefly. Clay here filled me in on the important details."

"He did?" Her head snapped around. "You did?"

"I needed to know my enemy, that's all," Clay said.

Sandy Lynn felt her stomach churn and needed every ounce of self-control to lift her chin and insist, "*My* enemy, you mean."

Actual pain followed when she saw Clay cradle the side of his jaw with one hand. "Kinda feels like mine, too."

"Well, he isn't. I appreciate your concern, really I do, but truth be told, my problems are not yours." *Neither am I*, she added to herself, ruing the reality of that thought. Embarrassment still lingered when she recalled the way she'd wept and begged Clay to take her away with him when he'd announced that he was joining the air force and leaving Springfield.

The astonished expression on his youthful face that night was burned into her memory. *And now?* Sandy Lynn looked at Clay, really looked at him. If she let herself imagine what she saw in his eyes now, she might suspect he actually cared for her. Well, so what? He'd had his chance and had left her in tears.

She bit her lower lip, remembering the way she'd turned unrequited love into loathing and had convinced herself that the only escape from the foster system, other than waiting to age out, was a quick marriage. At that point, had she been thinking clearly, she knew she wouldn't have believed the lies of a man like Charles. But she'd been hurting. Wanting to hurt back. And spite had led her to make the biggest mistake of her short life. An error that had ended up costing her the kind of happy future she could now only dream about.

One thing was certain. She was not going to repeat that terrible choice; nor was she going to let herself fall for another man, especially not Clay Danforth. Even if he had changed his mind about her, which was far from a proven fact, she didn't intend to let him into her life or into her heart again.

Charles's abuse had hurt, yes, but nothing had ever caused the kind of deep, lasting pain that she'd felt watching Clay drive away when she was barely sixteen.

Nobody had ever loved her enough to stay. Not then and not now.

FIVE

"There's no way you can go back to that apartment," Clay insisted.

Abe agreed with a nod. "He's right."

"Fine. Where do you expect me to live? It's snowing. I can't very well pitch a tent in the park."

Seeing the set of Sandy Lynn's jaw, Clay shook his head slowly. This woman was not only stubborn beyond reason, she was sadly deluded if she thought she'd be safe anywhere until her enemies were apprehended and charged.

"When does school start again?"

"After the first of the year."

"That's no help. You need to be around people, not sitting alone in your apartment."

"Do you think I haven't figured out that we can't go home? That's not the problem."

"Then what is?"

"Money. How much do you think teachers earn? Or nurses, although Enid's in better financial shape than I am. I'm still paying off student loans and she has bills, too. There's no way we can afford to walk away from our apartment."

Abe elbowed Clay. "How long is your old place paid for?"

"Another couple of weeks, but last I heard it was sealed by the department."

"Maybe I can get them to release it, and the ladies can stay there for a short time. It's worth a shot."

"Try if you want," Clay said, making a face. "I'm not holding my breath."

"Whoa. Hold it, guys. I never agreed to moving anywhere," Sandy Lynn said. "Particularly not into a crime scene."

Shaking his head, Clay explained. "My place is clean. There's nothing there for them to find—unless somebody planted more evidence after I left. I doubt they bothered to access more than my car." He made a face. "Why do you think I'm riding a motorcycle in the middle of winter?"

"Ah." She appeared lost in thought before adding, "I'd wondered who the bike parked next to my car belonged to."

"Are you hinting you'd like a ride?" Abe asked, grinning.

"Uh-uh. No way. Charles and a bunch of his buddies used to ride together and he made me learn, but I've never enjoyed it."

"Really? Why not?" Clay was curious.

"Because he used it as another way to make my life miserable, I guess. If he couldn't scare me one way, he'd terrify me another. The knife is new, though."

All Clay could do was shake his head. "You still think it was him at your apartment? Even after Abe checked with the prison?"

"I can't help it. That voice made the hair on my neck stand up."

"Okay. If you say so." Clay decided not to argue this time. If she was wrong, no harm done. If Hood was somehow behind the attacks, even if he didn't carry them out in person, it was just as well that Sandy Lynn stayed on edge. The more aware she was of her surroundings, the better he liked it, particularly because he wasn't going to be able to defend her 24/7.

Abe reached over and patted Clay's shoulder. "Okay. See you later. You won't care if I run over to the station and use their system to do a little more research, will you? That way I can print out my findings instead of having to read them on my phone."

"Fine with me. We're staying put until Enid gets out of surgery."

"And longer if I want to," Sandy Lynn added as Abe left them. "We came over in my car so I won't have to leave until I'm ready."

"You wouldn't strand me here, would you?" he asked with a lopsided smile.

The expression on her face would have been laughable if the situation wasn't so serious. Finally she said, "No. I suppose I can't do that after you've been so helpful." Her left eyebrow rose up higher than the right. "Just don't start giving me orders, okay?"

He didn't answer right away. This was the second time she'd criticized him for being too bossy, and for the life of him he couldn't understand where she'd gotten that idea. If anything, he'd cut her slack, particularly when she was a confused, lost, angry foster kid. Coming from a stable home himself, he knew he couldn't truly identify with her, yet he'd done his best to empathize and support both Sandy Lynn and the others housed next door to his family. His mother had been supportive, of course. It was his father who kept warning him to give the other kids a wide berth, painting them all as unacceptable regardless of where they had come from or their past situations.

Clay knew his dad had had his best interests at heart when he'd made plans to send him off to college, but at that age Clay had rebelled, joining the air force instead and training to be a security officer, which had led to his career in law enforcement.

Correction. To his *former* career. What he was going to do with his life from now on was up to his union rep and attorney. The only plus he could imagine was that his job troubles had temporarily freed him to look after Sandy Lynn without running into a conflict of interest.

He rubbed his sore jaw. He was going to have to up his game if he intended to properly defend her. That was the easy part. The problem, as he saw it, was convincing her that she needed his help when she'd already informed him otherwise.

In his mind he heard her scream again. Felt the knot in his stomach again. Wanted to wrap his arms around her for protection. That was the worst thing he could do, he knew, but that didn't erase the urge to hold her close or the wish that he hadn't rejected her so effectively years before.

How did a guy go back? Clay wondered. His gaze met Sandy Lynn's. There was something special between them. There had to be. That, or his imagination was spinning out of control, which was a distinct possibility.

Taking a deep breath, he reached for her hand, touching it briefly before pulling away. "We need to talk."

"Okay. Talk."

"No. Not here." Clay eyed the officers lingering in the waiting room. "Privately."

"Maybe later. Until I know Enid is going to be okay I can't think about anything else."

Nodding, Clay blinked for a long second and turned away. The silent prayers he'd been saying since this woman had come back into his life intensified. Guilt for being secretly glad the assailant had attacked the wrong woman brought gut-wrenching angst. Her narrow focus was something he could grasp, because if Sandy Lynn was the one undergoing lifesaving surgery at that moment he knew he wouldn't be able to think of anything else, either.

Night dragged by, finally bringing the dawn, when Phoebe came to find them with the news that Enid was in recovery and expected to live. Sandy Lynn jumped to her feet and covered her face with both hands while the nurse delivered more details.

"It was touch-and-go for a while because the knife nicked her liver," Phoebe said. "But she's going to pull through."

Sandy Lynn wanted to hug her. "Thank you so much."

Phoebe chuckled as she sidled closer to Clay. "Hey, don't thank me. Thank our chief surgeon. Dr. Lindford is the best." She leaned in and looked up at Clay as she slipped her hand around his arm. "I'm going off duty. How about breakfast?"

Relief about Enid was paramount, but a twinge of jealousy peeked in around the edges of Sandy Lynn's consciousness. The intimate way the pretty nurse had mentioned breakfast galled in spite of every effort to ignore it. She could see that Clay was uncomfortable with Phoebe's suggestion because he was blushing beneath the shadow of emerging whiskers. Having rough cheeks and a chin like that should have made him seem unkempt but gave him a rugged image, instead.

Sandy Lynn sighed quietly and turned away. Truth to tell, he looked good to her no matter how he was dressed or how recently he may have shaved. The mature Clay Danforth was ten times as attractive as his youthful self had been.

Not that I noticed, she reminded herself with a self-deprecating smirk.

As Clay said, "Sounds like a great idea," Sandy Lynn felt his hand cupping her elbow. "Let's go."

Surprised, she looked up and saw him grinning. She peeked over at Phoebe and noticed a definite attitude adjustment. It didn't take a genius to see exactly what Clay was doing. Biting her lip to keep from smiling, she fell into step with him. The nurse was still grasping his opposite arm, but he was the one who had chosen to include Sandy Lynn. That was a special blessing. One she appreciated beyond words despite her earlier vow to keep him at arm's length.

I still will. Later, she told herself. After all, this was only breakfast. And they had a chaperone, whether it pleased Phoebe or not, so what could go wrong?

Clay stopped in front of a bank of elevators and pushed the down button. Before Sandy Lynn could ask where they were going to eat and plead for a speedy return to the surgery floor to wait for a chance to see Enid, he took care of everything. "We want to stay close and the hospital cafeteria makes decent food, right, Phoebe?"

"If you say so."

This time, Sandy Lynn did start to chuckle, then stifled the sound, which resulted in a noise that sounded like a strangling mouse.

Clay wasn't as polite. He laughed aloud and patted her on the back between the shoulder blades. "You okay?"

"Fine, fine. I'm just so happy that Enid's going to recover that I'm giddy."

Phoebe leaned forward to peer at her. "Is that what's wrong with you?"

"Among other things," Sandy Lynn agreed. "If you want the whole list, it's going to take longer than one meal to fill you in."

A bell dinged. The elevator doors whooshed open. Phoebe entered first, then whirled around, arms crossed, her back against the rear wall.

Clay waited for Sandy Lynn to follow, and he joined her, this time choosing to stand off to one side rather than between the women. If they had not been the only three people on the elevator, Sandy Lynn might have worried because she was definitely feeling malice in the air. Poor Phoebe was as mad as one of her third graders who'd had his lunch money stolen by the class bully.

Don't laugh, Sandy Lynn told herself. *Whatever you do, don't laugh.* Keeping a straight face would have been much harder to do if she hadn't recalled how disconsolate she'd been the night Clay had abandoned her.

That vivid memory was just what she needed to think clearly again. To temper her joy about the way this trying night was ending, to get control of her erratic emotions and make a friendly overture.

She smiled at the nurse. "Clay and I are just old friends. That's all. Honest. I'm sorry to intrude on your meal."

The hopeful look on Phoebe's face disappeared when

Clay commented, "Nonsense. You're not intruding on a thing. It's just breakfast and we're all starving, right?"

Sandy Lynn said, "Right." Phoebe merely glared.

As far as Clay was concerned, staying alert to danger was his number-one priority. Secondarily, he needed to make peace with the veteran nurse. Though he hadn't even thought of Phoebe since he'd been back in Springfield, he figured it was not a good idea to say so. He wasn't going to lie about it, but there was no need to be cruel.

The cafeteria was getting busier as morning came, giving Clay the jitters. "Would you like more coffee?" he asked, hoping to keep Sandy Lynn from leaving to refill her empty mug.

She pushed away from the table. "No, thanks. I'll just use the ladies' room, and then I'll be ready to go back upstairs." She looked to Phoebe. "Where's the closest one?"

The dark-haired nurse tilted her head toward the far side of the room. "Over there."

"Thanks."

Clay had stood when Sandy Lynn did. "You can go with her, Phoebe," he said.

Instead of taking his hint, she lifted her empty mug. "I'd like more coffee."

He could hardly tear his gaze away from Sandy Lynn as she crossed the room, weaving between tables that were rapidly filling with other diners. If he left their table to get coffee for Phoebe he'd lose sight of her, so he waited until Sandy had entered the restroom before fetching Phoebe's refill.

Hurrying back to the table, he sloshed a few drops. The nurse acted miffed. "Hey, watch it."

"Sorry." Remaining on his feet, Clay continued to watch for Sandy Lynn's return. He checked his watch, then compared it to the time on his cell phone. Very few minutes had passed, yet it seemed like eons to his uneasy spirit.

The touch of a hand on his made him jump.

"Why don't you sit down with me while I finish my breakfast? She'll be back," Phoebe said. "Probably sooner than later."

"No. I'm going over there to wait for her," he replied. "Nice seeing you again, Pheebs."

"Yeah, right."

Clay ignored her obvious sarcasm and started away. He'd occasionally wondered how some women could get along as friends when they saw other women as rivals.

That observation caused him to think more deeply. Was his nurse friend picking up vibes that he wasn't aware of? Could she be sensing that Sandy Lynn was secretly interested in renewing their relationship? She sure didn't act that way. Still, a woman's intuition might be more sensitive than his was.

Another conundrum? Yes. The differences between the way a woman thought and the way his mind worked were evident. Whole libraries worth of books had been written about the subject and still there was no consensus.

He didn't look back until he'd reached the wall next to the door to the ladies' room. When he did, he saw a tall man in a black hoodie standing near Phoebe's table. Surely that wasn't the thug who'd tried to harm Sandy Lynn. Or was it?

The man's broad back was to Clay, blocking a clear view of the nurse. Would Charles Hood—or anyone else—try to inflict harm in a room full of people?

Clay's fists clenched. *Why not?* The real question wasn't whether or not it was Hood. The problem was making a decision to stay where he was to guard Sandy Lynn or go back to Phoebe. He'd decided to stand his ground until the hooded figure grabbed Phoebe's arm and yanked her to her feet.

She shouted. Resisted. Then she reached behind her for the full mug and flung hot coffee into his face.

He yowled, let go and ran.

Clay was halfway across the room, chasing the thug, when he heard a scuffle behind him.

A quick glance back showed someone else, dressed in the same kind of dark clothing, dragging Sandy Lynn away in the opposite direction!

As he tried to pivot, Clay crashed into a small dining table, tripped over an empty chair beside it and landed in a mess of spilled food and drinks.

"Sorry." He struggled to his feet. Sandy Lynn was disappearing out a side door, and she didn't seem to be fighting to escape. What had they done to her? How could he have been so lax?

Fighting emotional battles already, Clay ran, dodging tables and slipping on the slick floor because his soles were coated with bits of someone else's meal.

He reached the door and burst through.

There was no sign of her!

SIX

Groggy though still on her feet, Sandy Lynn tried to resist being hustled along. She knew her brain wasn't functioning properly, and she kept searching her dulled memories to figure out why.

She'd been facing the restroom sink, washing her hands, when she'd felt a bee sting on her neck. The person she'd noticed standing nearby when she looked up wasn't familiar. Or was she?

Images drifted in and out of her mind. Pictures of the past, as well as the present, melded into a collage of faces and experiences. The faces in the mirror kept bothering her until she pushed them aside. One thing was clear. She wasn't supposed to be going anywhere. Clay was waiting for her at the table. Enid would soon be brought out of recovery. Therefore, whoever was pushing and pulling her away from them had to be in the wrong.

Wrong. That was it. Something was very wrong. It must stop. *She* must stop. Her spinning head and rubbery legs helped her decide what to do. She let her body go limp and slumped to the floor.

Whoever had been guiding her along released his grip. There was shouting noise in the background. A female was screeching. Was that *her*? Possibly. Probably. But she was so weary. So weak. If she could just sleep for a little while she knew she'd be okay.

The screaming tapered off. Sandy Lynn laid her head on her folded arms, curled into a ball on the floor and closed her eyes. When she opened them again, she was lying prone in a hospital bed and Clay was leaning over her.

She blinked, incredulous at the tender look in his eyes. "What...?"

"You were apparently given a sedative," he said as he took her hand and held it. "We weren't sure how long you'd be out, and without knowing exactly what you'd been shot with, it was risky to try to counteract it."

"O-okay." She saw someone over his shoulder and blinked rapidly to help bring the face into focus. It was the nurse who had not liked her. Now, however, Phoebe—*that* was her name—seemed to commiserate.

She was studying a beeping monitor next to the bed. "It's looking better, Ms. Forrester. We haven't gotten the results of your blood test, but since you're coming out of it, I wouldn't worry. Looks like you'll be fine in a little while."

Sandy Lynn was recovering not only her consciousness but also her wit. "I doubt that," she said, only slightly slurring. "I seem to be trapped in a nightmare of my own making. I'm afraid being *fine* isn't in the script."

She watched the nurse lay a hand on Clay's shoulder and heard her ask, "You're staying with her?"

"Yes."

"Okay, then I'll be going. Don't worry. She's in good hands."

Clay nodded. "As good as I can make them."

Sandy Lynn didn't try to speak past the lump in her throat as she and Clay were left alone. Relief and gratitude filled her. What she could see of his face through the veil of her own tears told her the sentiments were shared.

Finally she managed, "Thank you. Again."

A smile barely lifted the corners of his mouth. "I'd say it was my pleasure, but that's not quite true. I'd much rather not have to rescue you."

"Yeah, well." Pausing to swallow, she went on. "What am I going to do next?"

"Beats me. We'll think of something."

"We? This really isn't your problem, you know," Sandy Lynn said sadly. "It's all mine. I should work out a solution."

"Okay. What's the plan."

"I thought I'd start with staying alive."

"Good idea," Clay quipped back. "After that?"

She sobered as the weight of the future came to rest on her weary body and brain. "How long was I out? Have you heard anything about Enid?"

"She's resting. You may as well kick back until she's allowed visitors."

Sandy Lynn yawned. "What about you?"

"I'll beat back the cops who want to interview you, so you can relax until you feel better. I take it you don't remember much. You were out like a light at the end."

"Not really. I did see the reflection of another woman in the mirror just before I felt a sting—I thought it was a bee. I take it she gave me a shot."

"That's the doctor's conclusion. All your vital signs were okay, but you were unconscious."

"Lovely." She wondered how to ask him to stay

nearby without sounding needy. "If I do nap, will you arrange for a guard?"

Clay's expression hardened, and he got to his feet to stand next to her hospital bed. "Besides me, you mean."

"I didn't say that. I just…"

"You don't have to explain. I get it." He was backing away. "Sure. Leave it to me. I'll talk to the officers waiting in the hallway, and if they don't agree to post somebody at your door I'll give Abe a call."

Sandy Lynn's jaw dropped. She had expected Clay to confirm himself as her protector, not arrange for someone else. Clearly, his feelings were hurt and that pained her, but why was he acting so upset?

Growing sleepy again, she let her lids droop and sighed deeply. All this was so confusing. So impossible to predict.

Her mind drifted. Given so little information on who was after her, she tried to blame Charles again and failed. After that first time in her apartment, she hadn't sensed his malevolent presence or heard the voice that instantly gave her shivers. Had she been wrong to begin with?

She yawned again, covering her mouth even though there was nobody with her to notice. *Sleep. I need sleep. Maybe just a tiny nap, and then I'll get up and check on Enid.*

Eyes closed, she managed to think, *Thank you, Father, for sending Clay*, before she faded all the way past awareness.

"Look," Clay told Harper and Allgood, the uniformed officers in the hallway, "if you want to interview Ms. Forrester, you'll need to speak to her doctor first. Otherwise, you're not going in." Disliking the hard looks he was receiving, he added, "She's not awake, anyway."

"When will she be?"

Shrugging, Clay forced a smile. "How do I know? I'm not the one who knocked her out in the first place."

"So you say."

Refusing to back down, Clay said, "Me, and a cafeteria full of witnesses."

A taller, blond-gray, middle-aged man Clay hadn't met before was standing behind the others, holding a small tablet and tapping on the screen.

Before Clay had a chance to ask who he was, he came forward with his right hand extended and introduced himself. "Detective Johansen. I take it you're Clay Danforth."

Clay shook the man's hand, finding the grip firm though not punishingly so. "Yes. I am." He inclined his head toward the hospital room. "That's Sandy Lynn Forrester in there. She's been attacked more than once in the past twenty-four hours, and her roommate was seriously injured."

"So I've heard. What else can you tell me?"

"Not much. It all started when I heard a ruckus on the floor above my apartment and called 911. I went to investigate. A masked figure ran past me and escaped. I found Enid Bloom, the roommate, on the floor and called for an ambulance, too."

"That's all?"

"Pretty much." Clay knew he was scowling at the man and worked to hold back his temper. Johansen was different from the uniformed officers. Not only did he have more clout, he seemed willing to listen.

Again, the detective consulted his iPad. Clay wondered if he was actually reading anything on it or simply using a stalling tactic to make the suspect, namely him, sweat. Well, he knew their tricks. They wouldn't work on him.

"You say you live in the same apartment building as both victims?"

"Yes." Clay thought he should explain. "I didn't know Ms. Forrester lived there when I signed the lease, or I'd have found someplace else to rent."

"Why is that?"

Sighing, Clay briefly laid out their past acquaintance. "That's all it was. We lived next door to each other years ago."

"What about Enid Bloom?"

"I didn't meet her until she was injured."

"You're sure about that?"

Clay set his jaw and allowed his frown to develop. "Of course I'm sure. I hadn't seen Sandy Lynn for ten years. Not since I left Springfield to join the air force."

Johansen was typing. "I see you did well there. Security Forces. That's like MPs in the army, right?"

"Yes. I joined the civilian police force when I got out of the service."

"So, what made you turn to selling drugs?"

"What?" Clay was floored.

Johansen was staring straight at him. "Tell me about the drugs? Was Ms. Forrester involved? Is that why you moved into her building?"

"No!" He wanted to shout, to slam his fist into something or someone. Instead, he calmed himself and faced the detective boldly. "I have never had anything to do with the sale or use of drugs. Any kind. And I had not seen Sandy Lynn for many years, let alone had contact with her. We did not part on the best of terms and had lost touch."

One of the other officers, Harper, spoke up. "So we're supposed to believe you rented an apartment in her building by chance. Ha!"

Johansen shot the younger man a stern look of warning. "I suppose it is possible to have moved there without knowing where she lived, but you must admit it's barely plausible."

Although Clay didn't want to get Abe involved, he saw no alternative. "A friend recommended the place. I truly had no idea she was already living there."

"Your reason for moving was…?" The detective seemed to have a one-track mind.

Staring at the other officers, one at a time, Clay finally said, "My condo was turned into a supposed crime scene. Without a job I couldn't afford to keep living there, anyway, so I looked for a cheaper place. Finding one was not easy, and I jumped at the chance without investigating the other tenants."

"Are you saying you would not have rented there if you had known Ms. Forrester was also a resident?"

He nodded slowly, pensively. "That's what I thought initially. Now, I'm beginning to believe I was meant to be around when she needed me."

"The luck of the draw?"

Clay adamantly disagreed. "No way. If it's anything, it's divine providence that I was nearby when the attack occurred. If I hadn't been, both women might have been killed."

Taking his time, Johansen consulted the computer screen again, then looked up at Clay. "Has it occurred to you that some of your drug buddies might have been after you, instead? Maybe they got the wrong floor."

"Not for a second," Clay shot back. "I am not connected to crime in any way." Behind the detective, both officers were chuckling wryly, so he went on. "I was framed. Beautifully, I might add. I'd gotten a whiff of corruption at my station almost as soon as I transferred in. The next thing I knew, I was being charged and my car was impounded. Packets of drugs were found hidden in the car, so they locked me out of my apartment, too."

Johansen was studying him, assessing him. "Why aren't you in custody?"

"Humph. Because my chief is smarter than that. There were no prints on the drug baggies. Not mine or anybody's. I suggested he have the contents tested to see if the formulation matched any already in evidence and he found a match. Do you think I'd have done that if I'd stolen them from the property room in the first place?"

"That's the charge?"

"That, and possession. Once the chief suspended me, I knew I was finished as a cop."

"You still maintain innocence?" Johansen asked.

"Until my dying day," Clay insisted.

Harper's partner, Allgood, gestured toward the closed door of the hospital room. "Keep hanging around her, and that may come sooner than you think."

Clay whirled on him. "Is that a threat?"

"Nope. Just an observation. Whatever she's mixed up in is beginning to look more serious than your theft of confiscated drugs."

Before Clay had time to respond, the detective held up a hand to end the discussion. "Everybody calm down. We'll get to the bottom of this, one way or another." He pointed. "Harper, you stand guard on Ms. Forrester's room until she's discharged. Her doctor promised she could go home later today if there were no complications, so it shouldn't be long."

"Yes, sir."

Ignoring Clay, Johansen turned to Allgood. "You head on up to the surgery floor, locate Ms. Bloom, and look after her for the present. Am I clear?"

"Yes, sir."

Waiting to be mentioned, Clay stood ready to argue if he was told to leave the premises. Instead, the detective said, "You're free to go wherever you choose, for now. You should know that I plan to look into your case, as well as Ms. Forrester's. Tell me. Do you think they're connected in any way?"

Clay was taken aback. "Such as?"

"I don't know. Yet. But if you do recognize anyone loitering, I expect you to contact me or the department ASAP." Standing with his back to the uniformed officers, he handed Clay his business card. Johansen shifted his eyes to the left and lifted his chin almost imperceptibly, convincing Clay he wasn't the only suspect standing there.

That was a partial relief, at least. Regular patrol officers tended to band together against a common enemy, namely him, and they had, as soon as the trumped-up charges surfaced. Johansen was subtly letting him know that he had a chance of proving his innocence. That, alone, was a blessing.

As the detective turned to go, he added an afterthought. "And don't leave town. That would make you look guilty and we'd have to issue an arrest warrant. Am I understood?"

"Perfectly," Clay said. He had no intentions of running away. Never had.

A raised hand was the only goodbye he got from the older man. Allgood had already left to locate Enid's room, and Harper stood at attention next to Sandy Lynn's.

Clay started for her door.

Harper stepped into his way. "Where do you think you're going?"

"Into that room," Clay said with determination. "Move."

"Or what?"

"Or I'll move you."

Grinning, Harper folded his arms across his chest, standing like a soldier ready for battle. "If you accost a sworn police officer you can be arrested. Then what good will you be to her or her friend?"

"You're assuming you'll be around to press charges," Clay threatened, acting the way he'd sometimes had to when he was patrolling the air base where he'd been stationed. "If I'm half as bad as you all seem to think I am, maybe you'd better try to stay on my good side."

He wouldn't have harmed the smug cop, of course. Clay just hoped Harper didn't realize that. A bluff wouldn't work a second time if it wasn't convincing enough to get him to back down now.

Almost nose to nose, Clay stood his ground. "Well?"

The cop shifted. "You were in there with her before so I guess it'll be okay this time. Just don't try anything funny, like kidnapping."

Clay huffed. Arguing would be fruitless, he knew, despite the strong urge to defend his prior actions. Fortunately, Johansen's approach had given him enough confidence to ignore this latest slur. A lot was riding on the detective's good opinion of him, and the last thing he wanted to do was get into a shouting match—or worse—with any cops.

Sandy Lynn looked to be sleeping when he reentered her room, quietly closed the door behind him and tiptoed up to her bed. Her lashes fluttered and her closed eyes moved rapidly, signaling REM sleep. She was dreaming.

He pulled up a chair and sat next to the bed, watching, waiting, wondering how they had ended up as emotionally distanced as they seemed to be. How might their lives have been different if he had been mature enough to respond to her confessions of affection and stay in Springfield instead of leaving?

They wouldn't have made a good couple, not then, and probably not now, either. Nevertheless, he did care for her. Describing his feelings was a lot harder than acknowledging them. He didn't see her as a little sister. He never had. A friend, yes. Perhaps a good one, although she had certainly complicated things by throwing herself at him as an impressionable teen.

She began to make soft, mewling sounds. Her head turned from side to side, making a bigger dent in the pillow. Her eyes moved faster and faster until she was quivering all over.

Clay reached for her hand to calm her. He saw her take a deep, stuttering breath and anticipated what was to come.

Sandy Lynn sat bolt upright, ready to scream and bring Harper on the run.

That's when Clay did the only thing he could think of other than clamping his hand over her mouth and manhandling her.

He perched on the side of the bed and pulled her into his embrace, speaking words of comfort and rocking gently back and forth.

"Easy, Sandy Lynn. Easy. You're safe. I've got you."

Feeling her tension ebbing, he whispered, "I'll take care of you."

To his surprise, she softly asked, "Who will take care of you?"

SEVEN

Sleep had brought enough renewed strength to enable Sandy Lynn to get herself up and dressed. While she prepared to leave her room, she mentally put together bits and pieces of the latest events, trying to make sense of them.

Emotional and physical weakness had kept her from resisting Clay's impromptu embrace. Nevertheless, she could not get the sweet memory to go away. How many times in the distant past had she imagined what it would be like to be in his arms? Hundreds. Maybe more. And yet, reality had far surpassed anything she'd visualized.

So why wasn't she more thankful? That answer was easy. What good were fervent prayers if the answers came too late? It was almost as if God was taunting her by sticking her in this situation involving Clay Danforth after she had already been ruined as a wife. Clay's wished-for big family was certainly not going to come from her. No children were, thanks to Charles's cruelty. Although doctors had saved her from bleeding to death, there were times, like the present, when she almost wished they had let her go.

Maudlin thoughts rarely crept into her mind and when they did, like now, she immediately banished them by thanking God for her life and for the children she got to love as she taught class. That was her life now, and it was a fulfilling one. She had a college degree despite being removed from her mother by social services; she was well-thought-of in the community, and she had a church family to depend upon and enough income to be comfortable. What more could she ask for?

The image of Clay's appealing face popped into her mind and refused to go away. She was in the midst of asking the Lord to help her cope with Clay when the man himself knocked on her door and peeked in.

He grinned. "Hey."

"Hey, yourself." Sandy Lynn motioned him in. "How's Enid?"

"Good, good." Clay entered, stopping a long way back compared to where he'd been before. "She's been moved to a regular room. Anytime you're ready, I can take you to see her."

"Really?"

"Really."

"Did they catch the people who have been causing all the trouble?"

"Not yet. But they will. It's only a matter of time. Police found a discarded hypodermic needle in the trash can outside the ladies' room. Abe thought they might get prints off it."

"Not likely, but I'm glad they're taking this seriously. I'd be a lot more worried if they weren't."

"True."

She slid off the bed then sat to put on her boots. "Surely, the attacker wore gloves."

"Yes, but maybe the one who provided the sedative didn't. It's always worth checking."

"Whatever you say." Keeping her eyes on her boots

to ease any embarrassment, she said, "I thought I heard you talking in the hallway. Someone mentioned drugs. Were you involved in a drug bust before you left the police force?"

"Several. Why?"

"Just that I'm glad. Even the little kids in my classes come up with dangerous stuff occasionally. They get it from older siblings. Or parents. The more you can get off the street, the better I like it."

"I need to explain more, to tell you why I left the force," Clay said quietly. "But not here. Not with Harper listening at the door."

"Fine." She straightened and grabbed her jacket. "Let's go."

Passing Clay, Sandy Lynn could feel a change, a disturbance of her inner peace and a definite uneasiness. Had whatever Clay wanted to tell her affected him enough that she was empathetically picking up signals? This sometimes happened to her if one of her students was particularly upset; however, it had never bothered her regarding adults before.

He pulled open the door for her and held it as she explained to officer Harper that she was signing herself out ASAP and would not be returning to that room.

"I strongly advise you to be careful about the company you're keeping," Harper said, giving Clay a telling glance.

Sandy Lynn chose to act as if she misunderstood. "I assure you I only trust those who have proven themselves to be my friends, so don't give it a second thought." She smiled sweetly. "I'm sure you'd rather be out looking for the men in the dark outfits and ski masks who keep assaulting me. Don't let us keep you."

Harper snorted and shook his head at her as if he

considered her the most foolish of fools. "Fine by me. I was assigned to watch your room, not you. If you want to wander off, I guess my job is done here."

"Why don't you call in and check with your boss," Sandy Lynn said, still smiling as her gaze darkened. "Tell him I don't plan to leave this hospital until I've spent some time with my friend."

She and Clay paused in the hallway, watching the cop walk off in a huff. "Can we talk on the way to see Enid?" she asked.

"Yes, providing there's nobody else in the elevator," he replied. "If your friend is sleeping, maybe a quiet corner of her room would suffice."

Stopping in front of the bank of elevators, she fidgeted, pressing the call button more than once.

"Does the elevator come faster if you hit that button over and over?"

"No. It just makes me feel better," Sandy Lynn replied. She managed a slight smile. "We're alone now. Start explaining."

With a heavy sigh, he began. "I guess I was kind of homesick and didn't know it, because when I heard of an opening in the police department here in Springfield I jumped to apply. And I got the job. That's when the trouble started."

She frowned up at him. "What kind of trouble?"

"I'm not sure who's behind it, but I have my suspicions. Being new, it was probably easier for me to notice irregularities in the way evidence was handled. I began to look into it on my own, and the next thing I knew, I was being accused of stealing drugs from shipments that had been confiscated."

"That's ridiculous. You'd never do a thing like that."

A smile spread across his handsome face and his eyes sparkled. "Thank you."

"For what?"

"For not even asking me if I was guilty." Clay cleared his throat. "You and Abe are the only ones who didn't."

"It's a no-brainer. Your character was always good, and I can't imagine you've changed that much in the past ten years." She could feel a blush beginning to warm her cheeks, and she was glad for the diversion of the arriving elevator.

After stepping in, she reached for the button to close the doors before anyone else had the chance to join them, then pushed Stop to temporarily suspend them between floors. "Is there more you wanted to tell me in private, or can we keep going?"

"Just that most of my fellow officers, including the chief, treated me as if I was guilty until proven innocent. I don't know how much of that was meant as a diversion and how much was genuine, but it left me no choice. Once I was suspended I knew my only recourse was to resign."

"You quit? Just like that? Why? Didn't you realize how guilty that made you look?"

"I knew I wasn't."

She had to shake her head at him. "That's all well and good. The problem is, when you took yourself out of the picture you ended your opportunities to uncover the real thieves yourself."

"I considered that. I also realized it would be impossible to do my job when I had almost no one I could count on for backup."

"It was that bad?"

"Sometimes. It took a couple of close scrapes for me

to realize the only way I was going to stay alive was to distance myself from the others. I just hope…"

"What? You hope what?" She waited as he looked away, apparently trying to decide whether or not to explain further.

When he turned back to face her and said, "I hope your problems aren't linked to mine," she felt a tremor sing up her spine and land at the nape of her neck, making it prickle.

Her jaw dropped. She didn't try to stop Clay from restarting the elevator. Surely he was wrong. He had to be. Because if he wasn't, she was making things much, much worse by allowing him back into her life, even on a temporary basis.

Letting the elevator continue to Enid's floor, Clay said no more. Though he wasn't sure he was right, he was unconvinced there wasn't a germ of truth in the premise. Ever since Johansen had brought up the possibility of a connection, he'd been mulling over the sequence of events and had come to no solid conclusions one way or the other. Sharing the possibility with Sandy Lynn had seemed only fair.

Straightening her spine, she stepped off the elevator without another word and headed for the nurses station. Clay followed.

"Enid Bloom is in four thirty-four," a nurse told Sandy Lynn.

Clay chose to avoid conversation until she'd had time to process his suggestion. It had taken him hours to accept such a far-out possibility, and he didn't want to rush her into deciding how to react. If she did think it was possible, he figured she'd tell him to get lost, which would make his goal of protecting her much harder. He didn't plan to give up, of course. Not in the slightest. But if he had to pretend to stop following her around, he would.

Sandy Lynn bypassed the uniformed police officer lounging in the hallway sipping coffee and eased open the door to Enid's room. Clay was right behind her. He shot a menacing look at Allgood just in case he was thinking of stopping them.

The door closed with a quiet whoosh. Sandy Lynn approached the bed with caution. Enid's eyes were closed, her breathing even. There was an IV dripping into a line leading to her arm where a needle was taped in place. A glance at the equipment told Clay that the patient's vital signs were strong.

"She looks better than I thought she would," Sandy Lynn said in soft tones. "Much better."

"I agree." It helped Clay to have her speaking to him, again no matter what she said.

"I think we should let her rest, don't you?"

Clay agreed. "Yes. Do you want to stay here or come back later?"

Finally looking at him, Sandy Lynn said, "I'd like to sit with her a bit, if you don't mind."

"Not at all." He let her choose a chair and pull it closer to the bedside before he sat down. It was difficult to keep from asking for her opinion. His old friend was bright and had an analytical mind. The conundrum was whether or not to request input.

Finally Sandy Lynn leaned back in the padded chair and sighed, then turned to him. "I think you're way off base."

"About what?" Clay leaned forward, elbows bent, forearms resting on his knees and hands clasped.

"About the attack being because of you. The first

one, the one that hurt poor Enid, happened before we knew we were living in the same building."

"True." Clay hesitated, then decided to speak his mind. "However, my friend Abe knew you were there. I didn't, but he did."

"What difference can that make? You trust him, right?"

"Yes, but…"

"But what?" One eyebrow rose as she began to give him a quizzical look.

"I suspect you're why he pushed me to lease my place."

"Why would he care one way or the other?"

"I may have told Abe way too much about our teenage years and he decided to play matchmaker."

"Ridiculous."

Judging by the way her expression changed, as if she loathed that possibility, Clay decided to ease her mind. "Right. I know that and you know that. Abe just hadn't gotten the memo."

"I trust you'll straighten him out."

"Been there, done that," Clay said. "It may have to come from you for him to buy it, though."

"No problem." She held her phone out to him. "Call him."

"It'll wait," Clay said, feeling his spirits plummeting. There was no longer any doubt how Sandy Lynn felt about him; it was just hard to hear from her own lips.

I should be celebrating, he told himself. After all, he'd been going to warn her off due to his legal problems, and he'd already told her enough to make her pull away, so why was he brooding about it? She had done *exactly* what he wanted.

But for a different reason, Clay thought, realizing

why it hurt so much. He'd wanted to be the one who pushed her away, for her own good. Instead, she'd declared her lack of affection for him in no uncertain terms. He didn't have to ask for details; nor did he want them. The Sandy Lynn who had once vowed undying love was long gone, and in her place was a strong-willed woman who knew what she did and didn't want, and wasn't afraid to say so.

In a way, Clay was proud of her. Oh, he missed the needy, lost teenage girl she'd been, but he was delighted to see how maturity had seasoned her. Had given her the sense of self-worth she'd lacked in the past. That was what she'd needed more than someone to lean on. Someone like him.

That was the crux of it, wasn't it? Sandy Lynn did not truly need him anymore. Oh, he'd stick around until the cops figured out who was after her and why, and that was all. Assuming he escaped eventually going to prison on the frame-up, he'd still have to relocate. There was no way he'd be able to get a job as a cop again unless he chose to return to the military, and he wasn't sure he wanted to go that far. There was always signing on as a security guard somewhere, he supposed, providing he didn't end up with a proven record of theft.

Clay sighed. Either way, he had to be glad Sandy Lynn was not interested in romance. Joy would return to him eventually. All he needed to do was convince himself that her attitude was the answer to his unspoken prayers for her welfare and stop feeling sorry for himself. *Yeah, right.*

"I think she's waking up," Sandy Lynn said in a low voice. "Look."

"I think you're right."

"Enid? Enid, honey, I'm here."

The injured nurse moaned. "Um. Rough night."

Clay was moved by the brave woman's comment, as well as by Sandy Lynn's tears. "Any night you survive is a good one," he said, trying for a lighthearted tone.

"Amen," Enid whispered before giving them a wry smile. "You two look worse than I feel."

Although he chuckled in return, Clay was cautious about agreement for fear Sandy Lynn would take his comments too personally. "We were up half the night fighting off the bad guys while you napped in a nice cushy bed."

Sandy Lynn interrupted to say, "Whoever hurt you hasn't given up. It looks like we won't be able to go home when they release you, at least not right away."

"I suppose I could nap in the nurses' break room if I have to."

"No need," Clay told her. "A friend reminded me that I have a paid-up condo close by. Nobody's living there at present and the mortgage payment is not due for another few weeks. You're welcome to use it."

Enid looked relieved. Sandy Lynn did not. She faced him with a sober expression. "Are you going to tell her about all the other attacks or shall I?"

"Other attacks?" Wide-eyed, Enid caught Clay's worried glance. "What other attacks? Was it the same guy who knifed me?"

"We aren't sure," Clay volunteered. "The police are working on it, checking fingerprints and closed-circuit monitors of the interior and exterior. So far, nothing, but they're hopeful."

"That makes two of us," Sandy Lynn replied, taking Enid's hand.

"Three," Clay said. "At least three of us. Four, if you add my buddy Abe." Checking his cell phone for messages, he nodded at both women. "If you'll excuse me, I need to text him."

Sandy Lynn shrugged as he turned away and he heard Enid ask, "Where did he come from?"

"Sorry. I didn't think to introduce you. That's Clay Danforth. He's the one who scared off the guy who did this to you," Sandy Lynn said, gesturing.

Clay froze with the phone in hand.

"Clay? Your Clay? The guy you told me about?"

Sandy's yes was so faint he barely heard it.

"Didn't he move away or something?"

"Or something."

A sidelong glance showed him that Sandy Lynn was trying to silence her friend with an index finger to her lips. His phone pinged. He began to read the incoming message and felt his heartbeat accelerating. The very thing Sandy Lynn had worried about had happened.

Pivoting to face the women, Clay held up the phone. "Abe has been keeping tabs on that minor prison problem for me."

"And?" Sandy Lynn and Enid said simultaneously.

"And, you were right." Clay pointed at Sandy Lynn. "Your intruder may have been Charles Hood after all. He's missing."

"What do you mean, missing? I thought the guy who escaped was some petty criminal."

"So did the warden. Apparently, Hood did exactly what you'd guessed. He exchanged identities with another man, who then took his place. If the other inmates hadn't gone along with it and covered for him, the ruse would have been revealed sooner."

"He's loose? You're sure?"

As much as Clay hated to admit that her worst fears were well grounded, he had to answer. "I'm sure.

They're all sure. He walked away from the work party half a day before Enid was attacked."

"I told you the guy said he didn't get the person he meant to hurt," Enid interjected. "I told you to watch over Sandy Lynn and you promised you would."

"I have been and I'll continue to," he vowed, wondering how he was going to manage it when he was persona non grata with local law enforcement.

Seeing Sandy Lynn press her lips into a fine, tight line, he added, "Don't bother ordering me to go away." He held up the phone. "I'm definitely not going, not after this."

And now he had an even bigger job, he realized with chagrin. One person to guard had been tough enough. Watching out for two people, when the second was also wounded, was going to take every trick he knew and the fortitude he'd learned in the military.

A good start was essential. Clay squared his shoulders. "Here's how it's going to be. I'm in charge. That's not up for debate. Do you both understand?"

Sandy Lynn opened her mouth. Before she could speak, Enid jerked on her hand and said, "We do."

"Speak for yourself," Sandy Lynn said flatly.

Enid was adamant. "I'm the one with the stitches and pain. That gives me priority. And I say we listen to Clay. Do as he says." She was staring at him with misty eyes. "I owe him, big-time."

EIGHT

Thanks to Clay's revealing intro, Sandy Lynn had had to explain everything else to Enid. By the time the whole story was shared, she was exhausted all over again, as if she'd just been rescued from one of her failed abductors.

Enid was stunned. "You're not exaggerating? All this really happened to you since that first time at our apartment?"

"Yes." She made a face. "It's hard to believe that was only one day and half a night ago."

"How time flies when we're having fun, huh?"

Despite herself, Sandy Lynn was smiling. "Yeah. But I've had just about all of that kind of fun I can stand."

"So, when have they told you I can get out of here?" Enid asked.

Clay interrupted to say, "Don't even think of leaving until a doctor discharges you."

"Hey, you don't have to threaten me." She pointed at the IV pole and tilted her head. "I know better than to cut treatment short. I imagine there are antibiotics in that drip, among other things. I'm not going anywhere."

"Good." Clay had kept his distance, and now Sandy Lynn motioned him closer. "We need to have a serious discussion about this, and I'd just as soon the cop outside the door didn't overhear."

Enid tried to scoot higher on her pillows, moaned, and stopped. "Hand me the bed controller and I'll sit myself up. Whatever you decide will affect me, too."

Sandy Lynn tucked a blanket around her friend's waist, lightly covering the sterile dressing. "Right. I'm lost as to where I should go to wait for your release." She darted a glance at Clay. "I don't want charity."

With her teeth still gritting from the pain of movement, Enid frowned. Then she nodded toward Clay, speaking softly. "What about the extra condo apartment he has?"

"No." Sandy Lynn was not about to debate. Her mind was made up.

"Why not? Did you inherit billions from a rich aunt while I was out like a light, or what? Neither of us can afford double rent." She managed a wan smile. "We're not all rich like Danforth, here."

"Not rich, careful with my money," Clay offered. "When I left the force I knew I'd have to cut expenses so I decided to sublet the condo and rent where you two live. It seemed sensible at the time."

"And now he's bummed because he discovered I live in the same building," Sandy Lynn added. "He said he wouldn't have signed the lease if he'd known."

Enid arched her eyebrows at him. "Flattering. Was there anything else, or are you quitting before you're completely ostracized?"

"I'm pretty much a permanent resident of the doghouse," Clay said wryly. "It's a habit of mine. And, as they say, no good deed goes unpunished."

"Cynical but with a germ of truth," Enid said.

Sandy Lynn could tell her friend was growing more

and more fatigued. Patting Enid's hand, she stood and leaned closer to lightly kiss her cheek. "Rest. I'll be nearby. I promise. I'll stick closer than your shadow until you're ready to go home. Then we'll talk more about where to go."

The electric bed hummed as Enid lowered the head. "I am tired." A smile quirked at the corners of her mouth. "I'll just grab a short nap. You two stay out of trouble while I'm asleep, and try to get along, will you?"

Sandy Lynn was amused enough to respond with, "Yes, Mama. We'll behave." She peeked over at Clay to add, "At least I will."

"That'll be the day," he quipped. "You don't know her like I do."

Eyes closed and breathing slowing, the injured nurse was already drifting off. Sandy Lynn hated to let go of her friend's hand, yet she knew she should. Part of her reticence came from not wanting to leave Enid, and another part was because that meant Clay might expect her to pay too much attention to him. Not that she was swamped with alternate choices.

Tiptoeing to the door, he eased it open and shushed Allgood with a finger to his lips. "Enid's sleeping."

"I figure that's normal. How much longer do you think I'll be stuck here?" the officer asked.

"If I were you I'd call headquarters and check," Clay said. "Johansen probably informed the chief, but it won't hurt to make sure he knows you're still here."

"Yeah. Good idea. Thanks." Allgood paused, giving Clay the once-over and scowling. "Did you really...?"

"Did I really what?"

The other officer shook his head dismissively. "Forget it."

"Gladly," Sandy Lynn heard Clay mutter as they

walked down the hall together. "Since I'm not going to go back to live in my apartment right away, how about running me home so I can pack a bag for myself and one for Enid?"

"Your place may still be a crime scene."

"I doubt that very much. I can call and ask."

To her chagrin, Clay disagreed. "No. Don't. The fewer people who know where you are, the better."

"You seriously think the police are behind my problems?"

"No," Clay said, wishing he sounded more positive. "I just think it's foolish to announce your plans."

Sending him a cynical smile she shook her head and pushed the elevator call button. "Do you always see villains behind every tree and rock?"

"Ha! Laugh all you want. Caution has kept me alive so far, and it's been pretty advantageous to you, too."

"That I'll have to agree on." Her smile spread. "So, what's plan A? Are we just going to drop by my place and see if we can get in?"

Clay arched an eyebrow. "Oh, we can get in. The question is whether or not it's legal. I won't do anything against the law and I doubt you would, either. If there's crime scene tape on the door I'll call Abe and ask him to get permission. If not, we can just walk in."

"Don't you even trust your best buddy? We'd save making the drive for nothing if you contacted him first."

"Let's just say I'd rather keep him out of our troubles if I can. He's walking a fine line as it is by being my go-between."

The elevator door opened on the ground floor. Sandy took the lead, donning her warm jacket as she left the hospital and headed for her car. Snow had stopped falling and the passage of cars had left slushy ruts. "I'm driving this time," she said.

"You were drugged. I should drive."

"And you were knocked for a loop." She sent him a look of amusement. "That's a lovely shiner, by the way."

Clay gently probed his cheekbone with his fingers, wincing. "It's a battle scar. I got it in the line of duty."

"That, you did." Sandy Lynn held out her hand. "Keys."

"Are you trained in defensive driving?"

"I've been to Saint Louis. That should count." As she'd expected, he laughed, but it apparently didn't lighten his mood enough to make him give in. As soon as they reached her parked car, Clay unlocked the doors and slid behind the wheel.

"Hey. No fair. Somebody needs to clean the snow off the windows."

He started the engine. "I'll turn on the heaters to melt it."

"Oh, for…" Frustrated and more than a little miffed, Sandy Lynn pulled the sleeve of her jacket down over her hand as far as she could and started to manually sweep away several inches of snow that had piled up, front and back. Clay's efforts would take care of any underlying ice.

As soon as she'd cleared enough for him to see to drive, she climbed in and slammed the door, rubbing her cold-reddened hands together in front of the heater vents. "Remind me to pick up my gloves, too."

"I think you'll remember." He hesitated a moment for passing traffic, then pulled out. "I want you to disable your cell phone. I'll get you another one."

"Why? I can't see how Charles could track me. I

mean, he may be vindictive, but he's no electronics genius."

The lack of explanation from Clay caused her to glance over at him. Instead of paying attention to her, he was frowning and looking in the car mirrors.

Sandy Lynn whipped around as far as her seat belt would allow. Since the snow had stopped, more people had ventured outside, evidently to take advantage of the respite. The street was crowded. "What? What do you see?"

"Probably nothing."

"Okay," she drawled, "then why are you making scary faces?"

"I'm not." Clay flashed her a lopsided smile. "This is my normal face."

"Maybe it's the black-and-blue eye socket that makes you look odd," she said, not believing that excuse for an instant.

Again he stayed silent. She felt the car begin to accelerate. The tires slipped in the slushy street, and they fishtailed several times before Clay got it under control.

"Okay. That does it. *What* is going on?"

"We're being followed," Clay said as he sped up, sliding again and again. "I'm heading for the police station."

"Finally, something that makes sense." Bracing with her left hand on the dash, her right gripping the over-the-door assist handle, Sandy Lynn did her best to anchor herself on the seat.

Clay turned corner after corner until she was unsure of their position. "I thought you said—"

A hard smack jolted her car and snapped her head back against the support at the top of the seat. She wanted to shout orders at him, to tell him how to get them out of this situation, but truth to tell, she didn't have a clue.

Prayer would be good, she reasoned, if she had the words to pray or knew what to ask for.

Survival leaped into her thoughts as she called out wordlessly to her heavenly Father.

The car was hit again. Clay righted it.

A harder smash followed quickly.

Clay hollered, "Hang on!"

They went airborne, diving nose-first into a drainage ditch.

Sandy Lynn saw his head snap forward just as the airbag engulfed him. The passenger side of the dated vehicle was not equipped with crash protection, so the seat belt was the only thing keeping her from flying through the shattering windshield.

Breathless and shocked, she just sat there, wondering if this was as bad as it was going to get or if their pursuers were going to stop to finish them off.

Long seconds passed before Clay recovered sufficiently to push his way out of the car with his pistol in hand. The street behind them wasn't deserted, and curious bystanders did seem concerned about their welfare. Several women were using cell phones while men yanked on Sandy's door, failing to budge it.

Clay leaned in past the steering wheel. "Are you okay?"

"I think so."

"Can you get your seat belt undone?"

"Yes." He watched her struggle against the tightness caused by the accident until she succeeded.

"Crawl out this side. That other door is too buckled to open."

"What about you? Are you hurt?"

"No. Mad at myself is all."

"Don't be. Those guys meant business. Did you get a look at them? I'm not even sure what they were driving."

"An SUV," Clay said. "Probably from out of state, maybe Arkansas."

"How do you know?"

"No front license plate. Missouri requires them, but Arkansas and some other states don't." Tucking the gun into the waistband of his jeans and offering her a hand as soon as she got close enough, he helped her out of the car and up onto the edge of the roadway.

A couple of women approached with empathic expressions, but Clay kept his arm around Sandy Lynn's shoulders and waved them off. "Somebody called nine-one-one?"

Heads bobbed.

"Good. Then give her room to breathe and we'll be fine."

"I seen it all," a nearby man said, gesturing. "I was gettin' ready to back out of my driveway when you come past like you was goin' to a fire."

Clay couldn't argue. "Did you get the license number of the vehicle that hit us?"

"Hit you?" He harrumphed. "All I seen was you speedin'. I didn't notice nobody else."

He felt Sandy Lynn lean more weight against him. "How can that be? We both felt the impact."

Nodding, Clay sought to reassure her. "Witnesses can be funny about details. Ten people may see the same accident and tell ten different tales about it. That's one reason we try to separate folks for their first interviews. One will call a car green and the guy who thought it was blue may actually believe he was mistaken and switch his memory to green, instead. They don't do it on purpose. It's just the way our brains work."

"That can't be right."

"Scientifically proven," Clay insisted. "Look it up on the internet when you get a chance."

"So, I might be all wrong about Charles being Enid's attacker? I can't imagine I'd make a mistake like that."

"You wouldn't under less stressful circumstances. But you'd just found your roommate wounded. Fear may have taken your mind back to a time when you'd been just as scared and filled in the sounds you expected to hear, namely Hood's voice."

She leaned away to look up at him. "You've thought this all along, haven't you? That's why you didn't seem too worried about the mix-up at the prison."

"I was concerned. I'm worried about everything that's been happening. The thing is, I can let my fear take hold of me and alter my responses, or I can keep my head and get you out of whatever nightmare is coming to life around you."

"That's pretty much how it feels," she said softly.

A shiver made Clay pull her closer and wrap his other arm around her, as well. It didn't matter whether she was chilled or just nervous, she needed to be held, to feel safe and cared for.

And he needed to hold her, he added, steeling himself to withstand the pull of his growing affection. Each moment spent in her company made his heart swell with forgotten fondness and left him one step closer to the time when he knew he'd have to deny his feelings and walk away for her own good, as he had in the past.

Leaving Sandy Lynn when they were teenagers had seemed fairly difficult. Now, he knew it was nothing.

Saying goodbye to her after all this was going to hurt worse than he'd ever imagined.

This time, however, he was mature, settled, wiser. This time he would sit her down and explain his reasoning so she wasn't confused. The way Clay saw it, all he'd have to do between now and then was figure it out and accept it, himself.

NINE

Sandy Lynn flatly refused to be transported back to the hospital in an ambulance. She'd backed up Clay's verbal report about their accident, signed the EMT's release form and ridden with him to her apartment in the back of a patrol car while the police had her car towed in as evidence.

"Don't bother arguing with me," she told him after the pair of patrol officers dropped them off, and they walked into her building. "Enid and I both need clothing and necessities."

"Who's arguing?" Clay shrugged, palms up. "I just want to go in ahead of you, that's all."

"Okay, okay." She unlocked the door and stood back. "Don't take all day." Gruffness masked her fear, and she figured it was better for Clay to think she was short-tempered than to realize how much she coveted his company. She definitely wouldn't have gone there alone.

As he sidled past her, she was almost overcome with the urge to grab him and stop him. Such thoughts were ridiculous, of course, but that didn't keep her from wanting to protect him the way he had repeatedly protected her.

"What's taking you so long?" Sandy Lynn called after him.

Clay didn't answer.

She tried again. "Hey, Danforth, what are you doing?"

Finally, he said, "I'll be there in a minute."

That wasn't good enough for her. Wariness warred with curiosity, and curiosity won. She edged her way into the apartment.

When she spotted Clay and realized what he was trying to do for her she was touched. He'd shed his jacket, rolled up his sleeves and was down on his knees with a scrub brush and pail of soapy water, trying to clean up the crime scene.

"Wait. We have a carpet shampooer. I'll get it."

"I didn't want you to have to deal with this."

"I'm sorry. I should have realized this would be waiting. Why didn't you mention it?"

He stood, shaking his head and drying his hands on paper towels. "What I should have done was call a cleaning service or our landlord and had them take care of everything before I brought you back here. We were on our way before it occurred to me."

"You're forgiven," Sandy Lynn said, hoping the response sounded like a quip instead of something more serious. "Tell you what. Let's both leave that for professionals and get out of here. What do you say?"

"Agreed. You go pack what you need from your room, and I'll get the cleaning equipment out of your way so you can grab a few things for Enid. I'll call the apartment manager and leave the rest to him. I imagine he's heard plenty about what happened, so he should be ready to fix the problem for you."

With a heavy sigh Sandy Lynn turned toward her

room, speaking her thoughts as if she was alone. "I don't know if I'll ever be able to feel safe here again."

"You need a dead bolt on the door, for starters. I noticed you only have the door lock and a flimsy chain. Almost anybody can push through that. The anchor screws are so small they just popped out."

She wheeled and saw what he meant. "Maybe that was what woke me to begin with. I know I was already awake when I heard a struggle in Enid's room."

"Possibly. I'd rather believe that than imagine he was able to gain access without making a sound."

Sandy Lynn wrapped her arms around herself and felt a chill working its way along her spine. The heat was evidently off in the apartment, which was probably for the best. "Um, why don't you leave everything for the cleaners and come with me? I mean, have you checked my room?"

"Yes, but I understand," Clay said with compassion. "This place creeps you out and you'd rather not be alone."

"I didn't say that." She made a face. "Not exactly."

A smile was spreading as he picked up the bucket of soapy water. "I'll just dump this and join you. Okay?"

"Of course."

She didn't want to even think of the horrible night she'd spent and all the mayhem that had been caused in such a short space of time. Truth to tell, her friend— friends—were all that really mattered. The rest of the damage was nothing compared to a human life.

Blankets and the coverlet remained tossed aside on her bed. Her sweat suit was crumpled in a heap. Leaving a mess went against her nature so she quickly put the bed in order, then went to hang her sleeping outfit in the closet.

Something bright and colorful on a high shelf caught her eyes and made them flood with unshed tears. Christmas presents. Waiting for Enid. Reaching up for them, she sensed someone behind her. Froze. Held her breath. Until Clay said, "What's that?"

Sandy Lynn whirled, two gift boxes clutched to her chest. "You scared the life out of me."

"Sorry. I thought you heard me come in."

His nonchalance irked her. "Last I knew, you were in the other room."

"You did invite me to join you." Smiling, he gestured. "Christmas presents?"

"Yes." She nodded. "For Enid."

The smile spread. "I kind of figured they weren't for me. Shall I look in her closet to see if she hid something for you?"

"Enid is crazy about Christmas, so she probably did. The tree was her idea, too."

"You don't celebrate?"

"Not the way most people do," Sandy Lynn said flatly. "I go to church if there's a special service, but I've never been into all the decorating nonsense."

"Why not?"

"Humph." Sandy Lynn was pensive. "You really don't know? Think back. Remember the first time I showed up to stay with the family next door to you?"

"Was it the holiday season?"

"Oh, yeah. Big-time. There I was, stuck in a house with strangers while my mother went to jail to detox and my dad hit the road without me. I didn't even try to pretend I was enjoying myself. I sulked through Christmas and half the next year."

"You didn't seem all that unhappy to me."

"Then I deserve a trophy for acting. I was miserable."

His voice lowered, softened. "I'm sorry."

"Don't be." She squared her shoulders and lifted her chin. "It forced me to face the fact that life would never be the same as it had been when I was little. That wasn't a bad thing, it just soured me on the kind of picture-postcard holiday fun that everybody else seemed to be having. You know what I mean. The happy family seated around a big dinner table with a turkey and fixings ready to eat while a lighted Christmas tree twinkles in the background."

"That's mostly a Norman Rockwell fantasy," Clay countered. "A lot of us try to recreate that scene and fail. It's not the decorations, it's who you're with. Families don't have to be big to be loving."

"Small ones aren't loving, either."

"That can change, Sandy. People can change. Your father and mother made mistakes, but that doesn't mean you can't find joy for yourself."

She might have argued if she'd felt she could speak without bursting into tears. Instead, she pushed past him, tossed the gifts onto her bed and stripped her pillow of its case to use as a tote. Neither of her parents cared about her. If they had they would have at least tried to keep in touch. As things stood, she wasn't even sure they were still living, and although she had done her best to convince herself she didn't care one way or the other, she grieved the loss.

I will not cry, I will not cry. She kept telling herself that even after Clay left the room. Self-pity was an ugly thing. She had a dear friend whose life had been spared, she had a job she loved, a roof over her head and enough to eat. These were blessings others might not enjoy, and she was wrong to let dour memories rule her.

"I'm thankful for all the gifts You've given me, Fa-

ther," she prayed softly. "Forgive me for not being satisfied."

The pillowcase was stuffed with clothing and toi-
letries in mere minutes. Grabbing it like Santa's sack
she threw it over her shoulder and scooped up the gifts.

"Okay, I'm ready to do Enid's room," she called out
from the hallway.

There was no answer. Not even a whisper.

The bedroom door stood open. She peered in.

Clay wasn't there!

Cell phone in hand, Clay had made his way to the
top of the staircase to wait for Abe and the crime scene
techs he'd just summoned. They wouldn't respond with
sirens, of course, and he had placed himself to keep
close watch on the apartment door. At this point he
supposed it was futile to try to keep Sandy Lynn from
seeing any more disturbing clues, but something inside
him insisted he make an attempt.

The gravity of what she had confessed about her
youthful disappointments had hit him hard. How could
he have missed seeing the signs back then? He supposed that being eighteen had had a lot to do with it.
Scientists had proven that the human brain wasn't fully
developed until a person was in his mid-twenties, although women reportedly matured ahead of men, so
he guessed he could give himself a pass. Then, not
now. Now he felt her distress keenly, and it was doing
strange things to him.

Take celebrating Christmas, for instance. Look at all
Sandy Lynn was missing. At least she hadn't given up
on the spiritual significance. That was a relief. But the
rest? Feeling as if he had failed her terribly in the past,
Clay wondered if it would be possible to make up for

it this year. Maybe, providing they were still together in another week when the day came. His fondest wish was that Enid would be discharged to join them. If not, perhaps they could visit her in the hospital and do a little celebrating there.

The door on the ground floor opened and Abe entered, accompanied by a uniformed patrol officer. Clay gave silent thanks that it was Tucker, not Allgood or Harper, as the men climbed the stairs and he greeted them.

"I was helping Ms. Forrester pack a few things for her friend and noticed something I think Forensics missed. The area it's in looks pristine."

"We relinquished control," Abe countered. "Whatever you found may not be admissible."

"I realize that. I just wanted somebody to see it and take a swab. From where it fell, I suspect it may belong to the attacker, not the victim."

"You're positive it wasn't already tested?"

Clay shook his head. "I doubt it. The closet door was open, and it landed in the crack where the hinges are. It's only visible if the door is at exactly the right angle. Even partway closed and you can't see it."

"What were you doing in the closet?" Tucker asked.

"Looking for Christmas presents." Clay pulled a face and focused on Abe. "You won't believe what Sandy Lynn told me."

"About her ex?"

"No, no. Farther back than that. I had no idea she was so miserable when I first met her."

"Teenage girls are known for rotten moods," Abe teased. "I should know. I had three sisters."

"Yeah, I remember. Maybe I shouldn't beat myself

up so much over it." He took the lead. "C'mon. I stuck a business card in the door to keep it from locking."

As he pulled it open he heard a gasp, then a scream. *Sandy Lynn?* How could she be in jeopardy when he'd checked the apartment from top to bottom and stayed just outside in the hallway?

In four long strides he was back at the crime scene. There she was. Her mouth gaped. She covered it with her hand and took a shuddering breath, then dropped the parcels she was holding and threw herself at him as if he were the last lifeboat left on the sinking *Titanic*.

Clay reacted from instinct and opened his arms to accept her. Momentum from her frantic approach pushed him backward. He bumped into Abe, who then hit Tucker, and the four almost landed in a heap on the floor.

Recovering his balance, Clay asked, "What's wrong? Why did you scream?"

She simply held tight with her head turned and her cheek resting on his chest.

Clay continued the hug as he urged her to step aside and spoke to the others. "It's in the closet. On the door-jamb. If you can't find it I'll come show you."

Abe snorted a chuckle. "Looks like you have your hands full, buddy. Tucker and I will manage."

Because his own breathing had sped to match Sandy's, Clay agreed. As soon as he'd guided her out into the living room, he asked, "What's wrong? Why did you scream?"

"You—you were gone. You'd promised you'd stay with me and then you didn't."

"I was close by. Right out in the hall, waiting for assistance."

Her eyes glistened as she leaned away to watch his

face. "Never, ever make a promise if you don't intend to keep it."

"I was. I was just…"

She silenced him with a look. "Never. Promise. Me. Anything. Again. Got that? Because I won't believe you. Do you have any idea how scared I was? Huh? Do you? I thought something awful had happened to you. And then, when I heard the door open…"

Clay spread his arms and gently grasped both her shoulders. "I'm sorry. I should have let you know what I was doing. I didn't abandon you. I noticed a new clue, one that may tell us whether Charles Hood was ever here, and I fixed the front door so I could get back in. I had to call for backup because I'm not authorized to collect samples."

Sensing a slight relaxation, he loosened his grip and urged her toward a seat on the couch. Judging by the way she plopped down, she'd begun to come to her senses. Tears were rolling down her cheeks.

She dashed them away. "You found another clue?"

"Pretty sure I did. Enid was injured close to where she fell, but you were swinging a club. Either you wounded him or he cut himself when he was stabbing her and the jolt of the golf club sent drops of blood flying into the closet. That's what I found."

"So it may be Charles's, not Enid's?"

"Maybe. Only one way to tell for sure. Abe is taking a swab and Tucker is along as a witness so nobody can accuse me of tampering again."

"Th-that, too?" she stuttered.

"They keep coming up with new charges. It started with the drugs planted in my car. I thought that was all, but Abe tells me some of my other evidence gathering is being questioned, too."

"What does that mean?"

Clay leaned in to speak intimately without touching her again. "It may mean that some of my good arrests get thrown out of court. And that's only here. If my previous department is eventually involved, I may be charged up there, too."

"That's ridiculous!"

It didn't escape his attention that Sandy Lynn had grasped his closest hand. He could feel her pulse pounding through her fingertips and sensed his own beginning to keep pace so he broke away and stood. "That's why I need to prove my innocence quickly."

"How?" Her gaze darted to the bedroom where the other two cops were working. "Is anybody on your side?"

"Abe is. And I think Tucker may be, too. I'm sure there are others, but they may be afraid to speak and wind up on the wrong side of the frame. Right now, it's just me."

"And me," Sandy Lynn said. "I believe you're innocent."

"So you've said. I hope you keep thinking that, because there's a chance my situation may get worse, particularly if these initial charges don't stick and they keep trying."

"Have you talked to your chief about it?"

Clay nodded. "Yeah. He would have arrested me if he'd thought I was guilty. But he has to handle the case by the book. That means Internal Affairs is involved, too."

"They should be unbiased, right?"

There was so much hope in her expression Clay hated to ruin it with his personal opinion. Nevertheless, he felt he owed her the truth. "You'd think so. The problem is how far the connections go. It was so easy for me to spot irregularities in the station I have to wonder how many others were aware or even involved. That has the potential to be a lucrative sideline, and some officers may have been tempted through need as well as greed."

"That is so sad."

"Spoken like a private citizen. It's a lot more than sad. It's criminal. And exposing theft and graft can prove lethal if too many are involved." Clay paused and waited for the full impact of his statement to awaken her defensive instincts. It didn't take long.

"The other incidents? You think they could have been about you instead of me?" She was on her feet, starting to pace. "No. No way. Think about it. They kidnapped me, not you. They wrecked my car, not yours."

"And they also knew I'd try to help you, follow you, stay involved no matter what. What if that's what they were counting on?"

The wider her eyes got, the more he wanted to pull her back into his arms and offer comfort. Parting her lips, she started to speak, then paled and stopped. "No."

"Yes. Either way, your welfare is in jeopardy. If it's Hood and some of his prison buddies who are after you, there's no telling what they'll do."

Sandy Lynn stared, trembling. "But if the evil comes from your side of this human equation, the only way they can hope to prove you meant to harm me is if I'm not alive to testify otherwise."

This time, seeing how deeply she was affected by her dire conclusion, Clay stepped forward and opened his arms.

To his dismay, Sandy Lynn turned away and headed

back into Enid's room. It didn't matter that he agreed with her that they should put a stop to any notion of growing closer. It still hurt. A lot.

TEN

Sandy Lynn couldn't decide who to be mad at. She had plenty of choices, including herself. That was the worst thing about making mistakes; the consequences tended to follow you throughout your life. The way she saw it, once she recognized an error it became her responsibility to avoid repeating it. Sometimes doing that was easy. Sometimes, as in the case of her feelings for Clay Danforth, it got harder as the years passed. How much better it would have been if she had never encountered him again.

But then she might not be alive to fret over what to do next, she reasoned, growing ashamed for wishing he hadn't stepped back into her life. If God had sent him to help her, she should be grateful.

Or I could be imagining things, Sandy Lynn concluded. That was more likely. Her practical nature seemed to have vanished the instant she'd seen Clay standing in her doorway, armed and ready to defend her. That picture refused to go away. Yeah. Kind of like the real thing who kept showing up in the nick of time.

She waited until Abe and Tucker left Enid's room, then took more care choosing clothing items for her friend than she had for herself, knowing how important matching outfits were to Enid. As far as Sandy Lynn was concerned, anything decent was acceptable. There had been a time when she'd cared about styles and fashion the way most teens did but that had ended when she'd left foster care and eloped with Charles.

The mere thought of him made her shiver. He had escaped, that was clear. Whether he'd risk his freedom and perhaps his own life to get even with her was not. The man might have a cruel streak, but he wasn't stupid. He must realize that coming after her was going to get him caught. At least she hoped so.

The pillowcase filled with personal items for Enid turned out lighter than her own because she'd chosen with such care. Sandy Lynn figured she and Clay could always return for more. If Enid agreed to change apartments or even buildings, as Sandy wished she would, they could simply pack up everything at once and have it delivered to wherever they went. In the meantime… She hefted the second makeshift tote and headed for the living room.

Clay was speaking on his cell phone. That reminded her of what he'd told her to do with her own so she slipped it from her pocket and checked for messages one more time before turning it over to remove the batteries and SIM card. She didn't realize he was paying attention to her until she heard him react.

"I told you to do that long ago."

"I still don't see your rationale, but I'm doing it. Okay?"

"I told you. It was to keep us—to keep you—from being tracked."

"And I told you Charles doesn't have the tech savvy," Sandy Lynn countered. She was making a face at him as she pocketed the memory card and gave him the other pieces of her phone.

His hand remained out, arm extended. "That card, too. You won't be needing it."

"I will later," she argued. "A lot of these numbers are unlisted and not written down anywhere else."

He rolled his eyes dramatically. "Then it stays here, not in your pocket or purse." That solution suited her fine. Let him be as brusque and standoffish as he wanted. The less solace he offered, the better her emotional state would be. Her breath stuttered as she recalled how he'd opened his arms to her the last time, right here, and she'd almost failed to convince herself to resist.

Curious, she sought to distract him. "Who were you talking to?"

"A cab company," Clay said flatly. "In case you haven't thought of it, we're out of wheels."

"When do you think my car will be released?"

His shrug spoke volumes. "We'll know more after the police are finished with it. I wouldn't count on it being drivable. It didn't look promising to me."

"What about yours?"

"Impounded. Remember?"

"Then we can catch a ride with your friend Abe, right?" She scanned the room and realized they were alone again.

"We could have if he and Tucker hadn't been called to a bad traffic accident on Battlefield Blvd. That's why I decided to order a taxi."

"Good thinking," Sandy Lynn said as she fought against moving closer to him to feel safer. Now that the apartment was quiet again, she was starting to grow more antsy. That was silly, of course. Until Enid had been attacked she'd always felt completely at home there, a conclusion that only magnified her current uneasiness.

Her eyes fell on the half-decorated Christmas tree and she sighed. Realizing that Clay had noticed, she quickly looked away.

"You can put up Christmas stuff at my place. I don't mind."

Sandy Lynn shook her head. "Not me. I told you how I felt. Unless Enid is out of the hospital by Christmas Day I don't intend to do anything special."

"Not even one sprig of holly?"

"No. Not even that." Sandy Lynn was adamant.

"Seems like kind of a shame."

"Oh? What kind of holiday decorations are up in your new apartment? You don't have any either, do you?"

"I've been busy."

"That's what I thought. So lay off lecturing me, okay?"

"I wasn't lecturing you. Not even a little."

"Oh yeah, then what was it?"

With a slow shaking of his head and sadness in his eyes, Clay said, "Suggesting Christmas decorations was my way of trying to make you feel happy and at home in a temporary place, that's all."

That brought a wry chuckle. It wasn't hard for Sandy Lynn to make up her mind to elaborate. "Don't you get it yet? The closest I've ever come to feeling at home was when I moved in here with Enid, and even doing that was hard because I didn't think I'd like sharing with a roommate."

Pausing, she studied Clay's face, looking for a glimmer of understanding. He still looked puzzled so she went on. "It's *me*. I have no roots, no place to call home.

I've accepted it, and I wish others would do the same and stop trying to fix me."

"I was trying to do you a favor, not change you."

"That's what you don't get. Enid didn't, either, not for a long time. It has taken me years to see that it's not in my nature to accept lifelong belonging. I tried. I did. But after getting married and having..." She broke off, unwilling to say more.

The stare coming from Clay looked like a cross between empathy and disgust, presumably over her choice of a husband. Well, too bad. If he'd listened to her, really listened to her back then, maybe she'd have had hope for their one-sided relationship and put off eloping.

Then again, there was no use imagining a different outcome. What was done was done. Irrevocable. She knew that as surely as she knew her own name. Even her faith in Jesus Christ wasn't enough for her to accept a second chance.

She'd heard Clay ask the cab company to hurry, but as time went by she began to wonder if their ride was coming at all. He checked his watch, then his phone, evidently saw something and clicked on it to read, then closed the screen.

"What was that? You don't look very happy," Sandy Lynn observed.

"Understatement, lady." Clay took her by the elbow. "We're going downstairs."

"Is the taxi here?"

"No. And I strongly doubt it'll be here for a long time," he said flatly as he grabbed one of the pillowcases. "Come on. We need to go somewhere else."

"Your apartment?"

"If we can get there without being stopped, that will

do for a few minutes," Clay said. "There's been another development."

"As long as nobody died," she said with a roll of her eyes, intending to lighten the mood and quell some of the nervousness that was passing from him to her.

He let go of her arm long enough to yank open the door and push her into the hallway. Instead of the usual stairway, he headed for the back way out.

"Whoa." She put on the brakes. "Where are we going? The last time we went out that way a couple of thugs were waiting for us."

"They won't be this time because they don't think we'd ride my bike in this kind of weather."

"They'd be right," she said. "I won't be getting on that thing with the streets so slippery and visibility bad, to boot. That's the worst idea I've ever heard."

"We have no choice. Unless the cab pulls up within the next few minutes we'll have to either ride or walk, and walking gives us no advantage whatsoever."

"Neither does being plowed over the curb like a pile of dirty snow," Sandy Lynn told him, hoping he'd see the logic of her sensible opinion. "We don't have to go outside at all. Let's go wait in your new apartment."

"We can't. Abe overheard a couple of cops talking to a suspect they'd brought in, and he thinks there are at least four guys helping Charles Hood. Maybe more."

"Why should that change our plans?"

"Because they're on their way here, that's why."

"You're positive?"

"As positive as possible, under these circumstances."

Sandy Lynn shrugged. Though she'd followed him down the back stairs to the ground floor, she wasn't about to hop aboard a motorcycle with him. No sirree. No way.

She halted before they reached the exit. "So, you're not sure? Then be sensible like me. Stay right here and wait." Resisting his tug on her arm, she shook her head at him. "Nope. Not going. Check on the ETA of the taxi. I'm sure it's almost here."

With a roll of his eyes and an expression of frustration, Clay pulled out his cell and dialed. "This is Danforth again. How much longer will we have to wait to be picked up?"

A scowl wrinkled his forehead. His eyes darkened and narrowed as he said, "I see."

"What?"

"The unit that was coming for us is still being held up by a traffic jam. That road is essentially closed. They can start someone else, but it will be at least another half hour before anybody gets here to pick us up."

Clay would have much preferred to ride his motorcycle alone. Too bad that would leave Sandy Lynn unprotected. He gritted his teeth and scanned the parking area. It appeared deserted except for a shivering squirrel huddled on an overhanging limb and some intrepid starlings pecking at pebbles through the slush-filled ruts left by passing vehicles.

Thankfully, enough new snow had fallen to obliterate the footprints of his prior attacker and blanket the place where he'd stopped her car and been knocked down, so he could tell at a glance that nobody else had recently passed by.

The comfort of seeing that reinforced how foolhardy it was for either of them to ride his bike in this weather. Was it truly necessary? Clay asked himself that and answered with a strong *yes*. However, as long as there was no sign of trouble, it probably wouldn't hurt to delay, just in case the taxi did show up soon.

Turning, he thrust the second bulging pillowcase at her. "Here. Wait inside where it's warm while I fire up the bike and make sure it's good to go."

"I'll come with you."

He blocked her way. "No. There's no need for you to get chilled before you need to be. Believe me, riding in winter isn't something I'd do for pleasure. Even with helmets and the windscreen it's going to be really cold once we get started."

"One more good reason to stay right where we are and wait for the cab." She was chewing on her lower lip, her cheeks and the tip of her nose rosy from the cold.

"It's just as foolish to stand here idle when I could be preparing for an emergency." He tried a smile, hoping it would ease her mind. "We won't ride unless we're forced to, I promise." The quirk of the corners of her mouth reminded him of the warning she'd recently given. "That's a promise I won't have any trouble keeping. I don't want to go slipping and sliding all over Springfield any more than you do."

"Yeah, right." Sandy Lynn made a silly face that brought out the lightheartedness he'd been hoping and praying for. Yes, she needed to be on her guard. And, no, she did not need to be so scared that fright disabled her brain.

It was a fine line to try to walk when a person fully realized what was happening, so he doubted that she did. Staying mentally stable and functional in the midst of terror was nearly impossible, even for trained soldiers or law officers. Whether she acknowledged it or not, Sandy Lynn's emotional stability was going to depend largely on him. It already did.

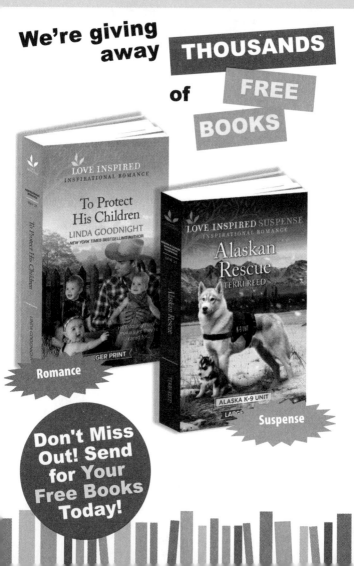

Get up to 4
FREE FABULOUS BOOKS
You Love!

To thank you for being a loyal reader we'd like to send you up to 4 FREE BOOKS, absolutely free.

Just write "YES" on the Loyal Reader Voucher and we'll send you up to 4 Free Books and Free Mystery Gifts, altogether worth over $20, as a way of saying thank you for being a loyal reader.

Try **Love Inspired® Romance Larger-Print** books and fall in love with inspirational romances that take you on an uplifting journey of faith, forgiveness and hope.

Try **Love Inspired® Suspense Larger-Print** books where courage and optimism unite in stories of faith and love in the face of danger.

Or **TRY BOTH!**

We are so glad you love the books as much as we do and can't wait to send you great new books.

So don't miss out, return your Loyal Reader Voucher Today!

Pam Powers

LOYAL READER
FREE BOOKS VOUCHER

YES! I Love Reading, please send me up to 4 FREE BOOKS and Free Mystery Gifts from the series I select.

Just write in "YES" on the dotted line below then return this card today and we'll send your free books & gifts asap!

➡ YES ⬅
– – – – –

Which do you prefer?

☐ **Love Inspired® Romance Larger-Print**
122/322 IDL GRJD

☐ **Love Inspired® Suspense Larger-Print**
107/307 IDL GRJD

☐ **BOTH**
122/322 & 107/307
IDL GRJP

FIRST NAME

LAST NAME

ADDRESS

APT.#

CITY

STATE/PROV.

ZIP/POSTAL CODE

EMAIL ☐ Please check this box if you would like to receive newsletters and promotional emails from Harlequin Enterprises ULC and its affiliates. You can unsubscribe anytime.

LI/SLI-520-LR21

Leaving both sacks of clothing with her, Clay stomped his way across the slippery drive and stopped beneath the open-sided shelter designated for tenants' vehicles. Nobody was home but him, as evidenced by the lone tarp-draped silhouette of his heavy street bike.

Clay whipped off the cover, shook it free of moisture and quickly folded it. Instead of stowing it in a saddle-bag, he laid it aside and began to inspect the motorcycle, beginning with a quick once-over and ending with an oil check. The gas tank didn't hold as much as a car, of course, but he also burned less fuel.

He swung astride, got his balance and started the engine. It gave a grind and a couple of sputters before roaring to life. There was something comforting about the rumbling sound, something that spoke to his inner man, as well as imparting a sense of barely leashed power.

With a grin he looked back at Sandy Lynn. She was standing just where he'd left her, meaning she hadn't taken his advice to step inside where it was warmer. Therefore, she was likely shivering already. Well, he couldn't help that. If her stubborn streak meant she'd be chilly, then so be it. As she'd pointed out more than once, he was not her boss.

Instead of revving the cold engine he cautiously let it idle to warm up, giving it tiny shots of extra gas to speed the process. Two helmets hung by chin straps from the handlebars, one containing a pair of gloves. Clay unfastened one, slipped it on to warm his bare head and noticed that the tips of his ears hurt as if being pricked by a thousand needles.

This idea is no good, he told himself as he donned the gloves. Even if Sandy Lynn sat close behind him she'd be very uncomfortable, perhaps getting sick or otherwise being harmed by the cold. He couldn't do that to her. There must be a better way. And the sooner he thought of it, the sooner he could have her safely ensconced in a defensible dwelling.

Clay turned off the engine. His bike fell silent. Swiveling his upper torso, he glanced back at Sandy Lynn. Although her expressive eyes were not as wide as they'd been when she'd spotted an assailant the last time, there was a look of concern on her face.

He checked to be sure the kickstand was down and started to dismount. Sandy Lynn's attention was not directed toward him. Instead, she was looking into the distance and frowning. She took several backward steps and braced herself.

That's when he saw and heard three mammoth motorcycles heading toward them; one on point, the other two flanking and positioned back from the leader. They weren't speeding. Their engines were idling with the rumble of leashed power so typical of machines their size.

Clay made a dash for Sandy Lynn, intending to scoop her up and force her through the door before turning his attention to defense. He was moving fast but awkwardly due to the slippery ground. Mental calculations told him he'd make it across ahead of the three riders. One more leap and he'd be there.

His left leg was extended, his right foot pushing off. Success was within his grasp.

He reached out to her and shouted, "Inside!" just as the sole of his right boot started to slide.

Arms windmilling, Clay fought for balance. Momentum carried him a few inches farther before gravity pulled him to the icy ground and knocked the air out of him.

He gasped as he tried to roll out of the way and failed, hampered by the icy ruts.

The lead motorcycle veered slightly, lining up to hit him.

Clay couldn't see the rider's face through the tinted face shield of his helmet, but he did hear the pitch of the engine rise to signal acceleration.

Everything happened in seconds. He was kicking at the icy ground, trying to push backward with his heels. The front wheel of the advancing motorcycle loomed larger and larger.

Something grabbed his arm, tugged on his coat and moved him slightly. Sandy Lynn? It had to be. Clay struggled to help her.

That was when he noticed the lead bike starting to lean. The sound of the engine became a high-pitched whine. The rear wheel had lost traction! He might escape after all.

Wobbling and fishtailing, the rider battled to regain control as the others rode past.

Clay gave a last kick, cleared the low ice berm and landed in softer snow as the rider cut the power, regained control, straightened his front wheel and followed his companions out of the parking area.

Only then did Clay look up at Sandy Lynn. Her face was red. Tears sparkled in her eyes and had started to trickle down her cheeks. What he intended to do when he stood up was scold her for getting too close to danger and risking her own life for him.

What he did, instead, was pull her into his arms—whether she liked it or not. To his relief, she came willingly.

Her cheek rested on his chest. She wasn't sobbing, but her breathing was irregular and raspy.

Clay's command of his lungs and emotions wasn't much better. As soon as he felt he could manage to speak calmly, he said, "Thanks. That was close."

"What?" she said weakly.

"I said, thank you for pulling me out of the way."

Sandy Lynn leaned back to gaze up at him, and the pathos in her expression tied a knot in his gut. Her lips were quivering and getting blue as the corners lifted. "Does that mean you're not going to tell me I shouldn't have interfered? Because if it does, I may faint from the shock."

All Clay could do was marvel at her fortitude in the face of trial after trial, threat after threat. A responding smile quirked at one side of his mouth as he tried to think how best to respond. Finally he decided to build on her wry comment. "Give me time. I want to think up the best way to tell you how wrong that was without hurting your feelings."

"You don't need to worry. I'm already getting a good lecture from myself. I can't believe I actually did that."

"I can't either." The smile spread. "What got into you?"

Sandy Lynn was shaking her head. "I suspect I may have a superhero complex. I have no idea where I got the courage or the physical strength to move you."

"Credit the ice," Clay said. He had been keeping one eye on their surroundings and listening for a return of their apparent enemies in spite of his concern for Sandy Lynn.

Now that the immediate threat was past he asked her, "Do you think that could have been Hood? You said he rode."

"Yes. Very well, actually, which may be how that first guy kept his wheels under him, but I couldn't see his face." As she stepped back she was brushing snow off herself. "Do you think they'll come back? Or do you think they were just messing with you because you fell?"

Some of the slush was melting into his jeans while the parts on the outside began to literally freeze. Clay stomped his boots and rubbed his palms together. "I'd come back if I was them," he said through chattering teeth.

Sandy Lynn nodded. "Yeah. So would I."

ELEVEN

She had insisted that Clay call the cab company one more time before she'd agree to stow the pillowcases in his saddle bags and swing onto the impressive motorcycle behind him. She knew what it felt like to ride "seat cushion" for the driver, but being up there behind Clay was so different from her prior experiences there was no comparison.

Arms wrapped around his waist over his damp jacket, she willed some of her warmth to him, as if there was actually a way to pass it along. Silent prayers for Clay and for their mutual safety spun through her head and found their way to her heart of hearts as they rode.

During the long years when she'd missed him and wished she'd made a different choice as a teen, never once had she pictured them riding together like this. The contradictory nature of the surprising occurrence struck her two ways. Yes, she was glad they were escaping and happy to be so close to him, even though the respite was temporary. On the other hand, she was certain that Clay would rather trust her safety to someone else, anyone other than himself. He'd implied that wish often enough.

Sandy Lynn tightened her hold and laid her cheek against his shoulder blade.

He reached up and tapped his helmet, then signaled to her. It took several seconds before she realized he was trying to tell her that the helmets were radio connected, and another few before she located the switch and activated their communications.

"Can you hear me now?" he asked.

"Yes. Where are we going? Your old place?"

"That was plan A. Are you still okay with that?"

"It's fine. I'd rather have Enid with me, but I'm not afraid of you. I trust you."

"As you should," he replied.

Even through a static-filled radio transmission she could tell he wasn't pleased by her candor. "I was just trying to put your mind at ease," she told him. "If you don't want me to speak freely, tell me."

Clay gave a wry chuckle. "Will it do me any good?"

"Probably not, but you can always try." She peered over his shoulder at the passing sections of Springfield and noticed less familiar streets. "Where are we headed, exactly?"

His reply was delayed as he carefully negotiated a right turn, then straightened the wheel. "My condo is up this way. A Realtor is negotiating a sublet for me, but nothing's been finalized yet so the place is vacant."

"You're positive?"

"Yes. I'm paid up until the first of the year. After that, I'd better have a renter or I'll be in danger of losing my equity."

"Equity? How long have you owned it? I mean, you just moved back down here, didn't you?"

"I bought it as an investment a few years ago."

That was a shock. "You bought a place here? In

Springfield? When you lived and worked in Kansas City?"

Because of her hold on him, she felt and heard him breathe a sigh before he said, "It's home, okay? Always was."

"So, that's why you came back?"

Despite a long hesitation, Clay finally agreed with her. "Of course."

Of course. It wasn't as if she'd expected him to say he'd returned because he'd missed her or had thought fondly of their long-lost relationship, which had obviously meant little to him. She'd known that already. So why had she let herself hope he'd admit that she'd been his motivation? Had her lonely childhood and rotten marriage taught her nothing?

To her chagrin, tears began to threaten. That was ridiculous. Clay hadn't told her anything new. There was no reason to be upset about losing a closeness she had only imagined in the first place.

The radio in her helmet crackled, drawing her attention back to the present. "What did you say?"

This time, his voice came through clearly. "Hang on. I think we've got company."

"What?" She couldn't believe she hadn't misheard him.

"Riders. Behind us," Clay shouted over the increasingly loud roar of his bike.

"Why didn't you say so?"

"I didn't want to worry you."

"I'd rather be worried than clueless. What can we do?"

While Clay's grumbling was incomprehensible, their acceleration told the story. Did he intend to try to outrun the others? Three of them? Even in good weather that wouldn't be easy. In snow and ice it was suicidal.

Sandy Lynn gritted her teeth and held on tight, hoping and praying Clay could go faster without losing control. She knew that her body position was critical, but beyond leaning with him into the corners there wasn't a whole lot she could do to help.

They began climbing a winding road north of downtown and lost momentum. Asking about their pursuers was out of the question because she didn't want to cause any distraction, so she swiveled to glance back.

That was a mistake. Clay began to turn left as she looked over her left shoulder, and the difference in their centers of gravity made the bike lean too far. If Sandy Lynn had not sensed the problem and righted herself in a split second, they would have immediately gone down.

She gave a little squeal as he battled to keep control. The rear wheel spun free long enough to throw a rooster tail of snow and slush behind them.

The motorcycle began to skid.

Clay shouted, "Jump!" as they tilted sideways.

Helpless to overcome gravity, Clay did the only thing he could—he put his bike into a controlled skid and laid it down in the roadway, letting go of the throttle at the last possible second to keep the weight of the rear section from crushing his leg.

He'd felt his passenger fall away. The following fractions of seconds passed in a blur. Careening along after the bike, he sought traction with his heels and elbows. Thankfully, Sandy Lynn wasn't screaming into the radio so he could hear the engine die. The motorcycle stopped moving when it half buried itself in a snowbank.

A hand lightly touched his arm, his shoulder. "Are you all right?" The words faintly echoed inside his helmet. The instinct was to answer with a nod. Common sense overrode it. Clay lay very still until he could make an internal assessment of his physical condition. As long as his neck and the rest of his spine were intact he'd be okay.

Sandy Lynn's voice rose. "Talk to me. Are you hurt?"

"I don't think so." He pushed up on his elbows, then tried to stand. The world was spinning on a wobbly axis.

Right there when he needed her, Sandy Lynn steadied him. "Easy. You took quite a jolt."

"Apparently." With a hand resting on her shoulder, Clay looked behind them. Their tracks weren't immediately visible because the fall had partially obliterated them. Although it was unlikely that the riders who had been following would fail to notice the part of his motorcycle still visible in the fluffy snow, he nevertheless hoped they would be going fast enough when they passed the corner that they'd miss seeing it.

"Hide," Clay ordered, reaching an arm in front of her and pushing her backward. "Over there."

Relief flooded him when she not only followed directions instead of arguing, she helped him wade through the snow and duck out of sight. By this time, Clay was so cold he couldn't stop shivering.

Crouching next to him and fisting a handful of his jacket sleeve, Sandy Lynn whispered into the microphone in her helmet. "I thought that was an old wives' tale."

"What was?" Clay managed as he did his best to quell his tremors.

"Chattering teeth. Yours really are."

"Anything to further the cause of scientific study," Clay quipped wryly. "Believe me, I'd stop if I could."

"I know. I'm sorry I teased you. It's the fault of my skewed sense of humor. When I get nervous, I make jokes."

"No problem," he said. "Just keep your head down and pray they bypass us."

"Pray? I have been. It doesn't seem to be helping."

"Tell me that a year from now when you have a long-term perspective," he said.

He heard her exhale noisily right, and she said, "Now *that* I *can* pray for."

Confused, Clay asked, "What?"

"Being alive in a year to be able to look back."

"Amen," Clay said softly. "Here they come."

Hunkering down behind the drifts, Sandy Lynn wished she'd had the presence of mind to run over to the bike and finish burying it while she'd had time. Now it would be foolhardy to show herself. Nevertheless, she was sorely tempted.

When she felt Clay's arm slide around her shoulders, she leaned into him just enough to demonstrate acquiescence. At least that was her intent. Facing possible injury or even death was altering her perspective, and she didn't know how to stop the change from progressing. Feelings that had been buried in her subconscious kept rising to the surface like bubbles of air trapped in the flow of a rock-strewn river at flood stage.

That was a good analogy, she realized, because her emotions were not only turbulent, they were unpredictable, washing over her and carrying her along as if she were little more than a dry leaf riding the current to who knew where.

The oncoming riders approached the turnoff. Clay's hold tightened as if he was afraid Sandy Lynn would bolt. "Do you think…" she began.

"Shush. Not a sound."

"But…"

He held his index finger up in front of the tinted face shield and hissed, "Shh."

Only then did it occur to her that the other riders might be wearing similar radios. If they happened to have them tuned to the same frequency, was it possible they'd be able to hear any sounds she made? Maybe. At this point it hardly mattered because she was holding her breath.

Closer and closer. Louder and louder the trio of engines sounded. Sandy Lynn could hear her own heart pounding in her ears as she tried to ease her breathing enough to mute her gasps.

Was that a sound shift? Or was she imagining it because she counted on her prayers for deliverance? No! She was hearing the Doppler effect for real. The three other motorcycles had passed, and the sound of their engines had altered in pitch and strength.

She made ready to stand. Clay held her in place, crouched behind a deep drift. "Wait."

It was all she could do to follow the order. If she had not considered it totally sensible, she would have disobeyed in a heartbeat and peeked out to make sure her deductions were correct.

Finally he eased his hold on her and she was able to peer over the piled-up snow. The rumble continued to fade. Their skid had been for the best.

"Okay," Clay told her. "I think they're far enough away that we can go." He pushed off and stood, bracing against her shoulder again in a way that caused Sandy Lynn to doubt his stability.

"How? Where?"

"First, we need to see if my bike will run. If it starts, we can take this side road to my condo, assuming the snow isn't too deep." He began to stomp through the high drift, following the trail they had blazed getting there.

Sticking close behind him, she kept her arms extended so she'd be ready to steady him if necessary. There were several missteps on both their parts before they reached the slick roadway.

Sandy Lynn went to the rear of the buried motorcycle and brushed snow off the seat and fender so she could get a good grip. Clay did the same to the front. A faint smell of gasoline wafted on the frigid air. "Is it leaking fuel?"

"I don't think so." Clay began to tug on the handlebars. "Let's see if we can pull it free. I won't know if we broke anything until I get her standing."

"Her?" Although Sandy Lynn was panting and fogging up the inside of her face shield, she was able to tease a little.

"A figure of speech. I was thinking of ships and planes. We call them women."

"Because they're needed and reliable?" she quipped.

Clay gave a mighty, backward tug, throwing his whole body into the effort and dislodging most of the front end, from the forks at the hub to the instrument panel. "More like because they're temperamental and unpredictable."

"Says you." It was her primary aim to keep him talking and assess his condition. He might claim he was all right, might even believe it himself, but she wasn't comfortable trusting him to drive at the moment. Whether or not she demanded that right was still undecided, but she was leaning toward taking control.

Together, they got the bike up and balanced long enough for Clay to set the kickstand. Sandy Lynn kept hold of the right hand grip while he raised his face shield, bent and inspected the engine and its surroundings.

"There's a dent in the muffler, but the chain's okay," Clay announced as he worked.

"How's the drive sprocket underneath it?"

Arching his brows, he looked over at her. "You really do know a few things about motorcycles, don't you?"

"I told you Charles insisted I learn. I think he got a kick out of showing off my skills to his buddies."

"You actually do ride?"

She fisted her hands on her hips. "Don't act so surprised. I placed third at a rodeo once. If the judges hadn't been so biased I might have won."

Watching his face, she could tell he was deep in thought. Rather than let him reason for too long she spoke up. "I've seen you wobbling pretty badly since you laid the bike down. I think I should ride in front and you be my passenger, at least until you get your full balance back."

"No way.

"I'm not trying to start an argument. All I ask is that you be honest with yourself. You aren't as stable as you were. Letting me drive is the only sensible choice."

Instead of answering her, Clay circled the rear fender and crouched to inspect the opposite side. Sandy Lynn couldn't tell whether he was stalling or actually doing something useful while he pondered her opinion, so she waited.

A shadow passed over them. Turkey vultures were circling, gliding effortlessly through the gray sky on updrafts. "Better get a move on, Danforth. Look alive. We don't want those vultures to think we're their dinner."

When he abruptly straightened, she was about to tease him until she saw him remove his helmet and cock his head. "Listen."

"I don't hear anything."

Clay reached for the handlebars. "You would if your ears weren't covered. Help me push this over the rise so we have more time."

"For what?"

"To get it running. Sounds like our friends are coming back."

Now she heard it. The muted roar of distant motors. Their pursuers must have eventually realized they'd missed them and decided to backtrack. And this time, Clay's bike was upright in the middle of the side road, black and silver against the white of the snow and ice. There was no way anybody could overlook it. Not even if snow was falling, which it was not.

As soon as Clay shifted into Neutral and released the brake, they both began to push. Progress was painfully slow in the slush and dirty snow. Several times Sandy Lynn's feet slid out from under her and she had to lean on the motorcycle to regain her footing.

They topped the rise together and she let the bike roll far enough to be hidden from the main road. Then she gave Clay a meaningful look. "Steady it while I mount."

"You're sure about this?"

"Positive," Sandy Lynn snapped back. "Do it."

The element that surprised her was not his compliance—it was the speed with which he acted. Clearly his mind had been made up. Good. That was comforting proof of his trust. Now all she had to do was live up to the reputation she'd bragged about.

Silent prayer for God's help went up as she labored to balance and hit the electronic starter. If Clay's bike had not been equipped with an easy method of ignition, she might have had to ask his help.

The engine coughed a few times, then caught. She throttled back so they would be less likely to be heard. It stood to reason that if they could hear the other riders in the distance, those men might also hear them, even at three to one.

Clay donned his helmet and swung on behind her. Although she had expected him to reach forward and cover her gloved hands to usurp control, he did not. When his strong arms slid around her waist, the sense of comfort was so strong she nearly lost concentration.

"Straight ahead until I tell you to turn," he said into the radio. "Take it easy."

"I can't balance well if we go too slow," she reminded him.

"I know. Just keep the wheels under us as best you can and don't dump it like I did."

Sandy Lynn considered admitting to having had a part in their spill and thought better of it. Chances were that Clay already knew she had contributed to the skid by leaning incorrectly, and right now her full concentration had to be on the road ahead.

One thing did bother her enough to mention. "They'll be able to track us if they ever find the corner where we turned."

"I've thought of that," he said as the radio crackled with static.

"What? It's hard to understand you."

"Yeah." More static. "I may have...when I..."

"Damaged the radio?" she filled in.

"Yes."

Although she did get his last word, nothing else came through. Even the static had ended.

Signaling him the same way he had her when he'd directed her to turn on the radio in her helmet, Sandy Lynn felt his arms tighten around her waist and took that as his reply of understanding. Losing a clear connection was not in their best interests. Still, people had ridden double for as long as there had been motorcycles, most of that time without helmet radios, so she knew they could cope.

She felt him loosen one arm and assumed he was lifting the face shield on his helmet. A tap of knuckles on the top of hers proved it. So did his shout. "Right turn coming up in about half a mile."

Sandy Lynn nodded. *Where?* She didn't see any openings in the piles of snow that had been left by a snowplow. It didn't help that the rays of the setting sun were shining right in her eyes.

Decelerating, she waited for some sign from Clay. He did point, but the show blended into a solid sheet of sunlit white so she wasn't clear on the exact place to turn.

Finally he grasped the handlebars and took over, his larger hands covering hers, and she lost focus for an instant.

The corner was upon them. She relinquished full control and they made the turn smoothly and successfully. Her relief vanished as quickly as it had come, leaving despair behind.

Directly ahead, in the middle of the side road, a pickup truck sat half-buried in plowed-up snow, totally blocking their path.

Sandy Lynn applied the rear brakes.

Clay backed off the throttle.

They came to a stop mere inches from a collision with the stalled vehicle. Clay ensured their balance by lowering both feet to the ground. All Sandy Lynn could do to help was add her tiptoes.

She raised her face shield and shouted, "Now what?"

TWELVE

"We'll never be able to ride through or around this," Clay said.

"What if we'd kept on going straight instead of turning the last time? Where would that have taken us?"

He was so disgusted with himself he didn't answer. Stalling for time to think, he balanced the bike and dismounted. "Get off."

"We're turning around?"

He knew she expected him to say yes, but there was more to their dilemma than she knew. Worst of all, finding that side road blocked had put them in a terrible bind—and it was all his fault.

As soon as Sandy Lynn was standing, looking at him as if she expected a clever plan, he started to explain. "This route was supposed to take us safely all the way. The only choices we have at this point are backtracking or going ahead on foot."

"You're kidding."

"Never been more serious in my life," Clay said.

Her sigh was plenty telling without the ability to broadcast over the broken radios. "We can't walk unless we're very close to some place to get warm and dry. You're still shaking and icing up."

"I know."

"So what's our best chance?"

"Heading back and praying we make the highway before our friends decide to turn around again."

Nodding, Sandy Lynn made a wry face. "Let's hope they're too lazy or too dumb to figure it out. Help me get this monster of yours pointing in the right direction so we can get out of here."

A certain amount of manhandling was needed to turn the motorcycle in such a narrow place. Clay managed better once he'd ordered Sandy Lynn to stand aside and let him work alone. She didn't look pleased, but at least she complied.

He swung a leg over and took the front position without asking. To his relief she climbed on behind him. It was too bad about their loss of radio communication; however, in retrospect he was glad he wouldn't have to listen or respond to her queries as they rode.

The hardest thing for Clay to control was his shivering. Parts of his legs and arms were already numb. If he didn't get warmed up soon, there was the possibility of hypothermia or frostbite, although his boots were keeping his feet warm enough to be functional. Judging by the way Sandy Lynn was snuggled up to his back and hanging on, she'd be all right. That was some comfort, at least.

A route that had seemed to take forever came to an end before he knew it. The four-lane offered them some cover due to traffic, and he was tempted to park long enough to seek shelter in a coffee shop. Anything to get a few degrees warmer before finishing their trip.

"How much longer?" Sandy Lynn asked in a shout.

"Fifteen minutes, give or take."

"Okay. I think I can last that long."

Clay almost laughed. He wanted to say, *If you can, I can*, but stopped himself. Fortitude would carry him through. It would have been nicer if he'd been able to feel his fingers but at least his hands worked well enough to handle the bike. That was something.

A stop for a red light temporarily quieted the motorcycle. Clay yearned to reassure his passenger, yet he didn't. Becoming complacent wouldn't do either of them any good, and considering the way cold tended to shut down thought processes, he'd need to stay as sharp as possible. So would she.

Temporary lots selling live Christmas trees lined the main roads through downtown Springfield and reminded Clay how close they were to the day of celebration. He hadn't made a big fuss over Christmas himself for years, but at least he acknowledged the holiday and used it as a reminder to keep in touch with friends and family. Since Sandy Lynn essentially had no family left he supposed he could understand her reluctance. Nevertheless, she surely had friends who would help her find joy if she wished to. What struck him as sad was her reluctance to even discuss the possibility.

Would she want to go to church, at least? It would be good for her if the threats had ended by then. Given the unknown qualities of their pursuers and the fact that they seemed to have insider knowledge of his efforts to hide her away, Clay strongly doubted either of them would be safe anywhere, even in church.

Logic insisted that his condo wouldn't be much better. So how else could he help her? They couldn't keep riding around on a bike. It was too cold, too dangerous in and of itself. He desperately needed his car back. And they needed to warm up. Dry off. Find shelter.

It took another twenty minutes to reach his destination. Slowing, he wheeled his bike into the parking lot behind his condo complex and brought it to a stop.

"Is this it?"

Clay nodded. "Yes. We'll go inside, warm up, get something to eat and talk."

"I thought we were going to stay here."

"You might, especially once Enid is discharged. Right now we need to concentrate on recovering from that ride."

"And then what?"

As Clay led the way past snow-blanketed bushes and up the walkway to his door, he wondered what his answer should be. Would be. Under normal circumstances he'd have stayed with her. But these weren't normal circumstances. Not by any stretch of his imagination. This was Sandy Lynn Forrester, the one woman who had managed to find her way through his considerable emotional defenses and pierce his heart. If he ever hoped to change their relationship for the better, he must make no mistakes. None. And that included confessing his growing feelings for her.

Clay unlocked the door and stepped through ahead of her to check the premises before they got too comfortable. "Stay by the door," he ordered.

"There weren't any footprints outside," she countered.

He couldn't argue. Passing through the kitchen to check the rear entrance he grabbed a broom and handed it to her. "See what you can do to cover our prints."

Sandy Lynn laughed lightly. "There's a big, black motorcycle parked out there. How are footprints going to matter?"

Wresting the broom from her, he headed for the door with it. "Never mind. I'll take care of the tracks after

I stash my bike. You light the fireplace. It's gas so you won't need wood."

Without waiting for an answer, Clay burst out the door, slammed it behind him and went to work. This method of travel had worked only because of divine providence, not because he was smarter or more capable than the men who were after Sandy Lynn. There was no way he was going to take her out on the streets like that again. If he couldn't get one of their cars released he'd have to rent one, which might be for the best, anyway.

After opening a narrow side gate, he pushed the motorcycle through, took Sandy Lynn's pillowcases out of the saddlebags, then fetched the stiff broom and set to work obliterating their footprints and tire tracks. The task wasn't difficult in the powdery snow.

Thank you, God, it hasn't iced over, Clay prayed silently.

He backed toward the front door, sweeping over his steps as he went. It wasn't perfect camouflage, but it was better than leaving the tracks as they were.

Instinct kept insisting they were not safe anywhere near Springfield. Common sense countered with reassurances that nobody associated with Charles Hood would know about this condo.

So, how had Hood found Sandy Lynn in the first place? Her name wasn't on the lease or the mailboxes at her apartment complex, even if she did get mail delivered there.

The first thing Clay needed to do, he concluded, was a computer search of her name to see how big a cyber presence she had. If it was small or nonexistent, perhaps she could stay at the condo while he provided a diversion.

"After I get warm," he muttered to himself, shivering as he closed the door behind him and propped the broom against an interior wall.

Sandy Lynn was hunkered down in front of the gas fireplace, leaning forward and rubbing her hands together. "All set?"

"Yes." He dropped the pillowcases on the nearest chair. "Dry clothes."

"What about you? You're colder than I am."

"I'll live. Just take care of yourself while I see what I can find in the pantry. I think there's some soup I didn't take with me when I moved."

"Sit by the fire and warm up first," Sandy Lynn suggested. "The soup will wait. You have to get dry." She was halfway to the hallway when she turned. "What about your clothes? I don't have anything that even comes close to fitting you."

"Don't worry about me. I think I left a load of work clothes in the dryer. I'll be fine."

Although she looked skeptical she didn't argue. Now that he thought about it, he actually might have left some sweats behind. If not, he'd make do by drying his jeans near the fire while wearing them. The important thing was taking care of Sandy.

As she disappeared down the hall, he called a friend at the station. Abe answered. "Matthews."

"It's me," Clay said.

"About time. I was going nuts worrying about you. Where are you?"

"My old place. I need my car. Will you see what you can do about getting it released? Talk to Detective Jim Johansen. He sounded like he was on my side when I met him at the hospital."

"Will do. Anything else?"

"Yeah. I'll need cash. Lots of it so I don't have to use credit cards."

"Whoa. For what? I thought you were planning on hunkering down till we caught Sandy Lynn's ex."

"I just want to be ready for any emergency," Clay said.

"You're not leaving town, are you? I mean, you know what the chief warned. They'll issue an arrest warrant if you split."

Clay gritted his teeth and turned himself in front of the fire to warm his other side. "I remember."

"You don't sound convinced."

"No, I get it. I really do. It's just that if it comes down to a choice between my future and Sandy Lynn even having a future, you know what I'm going to do."

"If you don't mind my saying so, that's nuts."

"Criticize all you want," Clay told him. "It won't change my mind."

"You'd rather end up in jail for a crime you didn't commit than take a chance of your old girlfriend getting hurt?"

"It won't come to that."

"Ha! Let's hope not, because if you jump off the pier into a pool full of hungry alligators, I'm staying on the shore and keeping my reputation clean. Just so you know."

"I'm not asking you to sacrifice yourself, too."

Abe huffed. "Right. It's bad enough you're thinking of doing it."

It didn't take Sandy Lynn long to get warmed up and change into dry clothes. She was in the kitchen trying to scrape together a decent meal when Clay finally joined her.

One eyebrow arched and her eyes widened. "Nice. Where did you get those sweats, out of the trash?"

He chuckled. "I'd left them here after cleaning the last time. Stuck them in the wash and forgot them."

Smiling back at him, she couldn't get over how good he looked no matter how he was dressed. His hair wasn't long enough yet to be properly tousled, but he was on the way to growing the kind of hair women stood in line to run their fingers through. Why he hadn't already been snatched up by some determined single girl was beyond comprehension. And that scruffy chin. Oh, my. Rugged was certainly becoming on him. Of course, so was clean-shaven and neat.

Warmth stole up her cheeks. What was she blushing for? Just because she'd vowed to remain alone for the rest of her life didn't mean she couldn't appreciate an appealing man.

Keep reminding yourself of that, Sandy Lynn thought. Clay had always been adamant about wanting a big family, lots of kids, and she was never going to be able to give that to him. *Which makes absolutely no tangible difference*, she added, disgusted over her wayward imagination. Fairy tales were for clueless children, not responsible adults like her. Not only would she hurt herself if she demonstrated a romantic interest in Clay, she'd be setting him up for the kind of heartbreaking disappointment she'd experienced when he'd rebuffed her affection and left to join the air force.

"I can't do that," she murmured, not dreaming he could hear her.

"Can't do what? Cook?"

Chin jutting out, she glanced over at him. "I can cook, I'm just not having a lot of success finding anything worth eating. I guess I should be thankful that you left anything behind when you cleaned out your cupboards."

"I was in a hurry. My Realtor was supposed to be bringing prospective renters by to see the place and I wasn't ready."

"Why didn't you come back to pack up the rest?"

The moment she asked the question she realized she already knew the answer. "You've been helping me ever since, haven't you?"

"Close." He struck a pose, hands in his pockets, bare feet on the carpet near the fireplace. "You *have* kept me kind of busy, not that I mind. It helped take my mind off my own troubles."

"How is that going?" She hated to ask but felt bound to.

"Fair, I guess. Abe is busy trying to get my car released so we won't have to ride double again."

A broad grin spread. So did her blush. "Hooray. This is not the best weather for that kind of transportation." Waiting for him to provide details, she busied herself stirring two cans of chicken soup that she'd opened to make a meal. That, plus slightly stale crackers, would have to do.

"I don't suppose you have any bowls stashed away somewhere?"

"No, but I did leave a few mugs. We can use those."

"Spoons?"

"Um, I don't think so."

Sandy Lynn had to laugh. "No problem. We can drink most of our supper and push the chunks out of the mugs with crackers if we're quick enough."

The fond expression on his face tugged at her heart even before he spoke. "You're amazing, you know that?"

"Absolutely," she joked, determined to make light

of his sudden seriousness. "Anybody who can make a gourmet meal out of canned soup with no bowls or spoons has to be a genius."

"Well, I wouldn't go quite that far," Clay drawled past a lopsided smile.

What a relief! He'd taken her hint and lightened up. *Whew.* No matter how long they were stuck together or how difficult it became to keep her emotional distance, she was going to do so. Period.

Memories of the beatings Charles had given her and the loss of her barely formed child flooded Sandy Lynn's mind and helped her shut down her emotions. If reliving such pain was what it took to keep from throwing herself at poor Clay, then that's what she would do. As often as necessary. Clearly, she was never going to be wife material, so why torture herself wishing for the impossible. It was enough that they were friends again. It would have to be.

There was no sound as his bare feet padded across the kitchen toward her, yet she knew he was there. Close by. He smelled wonderful, like soap and shampoo and… chicken noodle soup. Coming to that conclusion made her smile again.

"That's better," Clay said softly.

"What is?"

"Your smile. I thought you were a thousand miles away for a minute there. You sure didn't look happy."

"Happiness is too dependent on outside circumstances," Sandy Lynn said. "I prefer to concentrate on joy. That comes from the inside."

She felt a gentle touch on her upper arm and had to struggle to keep from leaning into him.

"What gives you joy?"

"Food," she answered quickly, brightly. "I am totally starving."

"Right." Clay withdrew to pull two mugs out of a high cupboard and placed them on the countertop. "Nothing but the best china for my guests."

"I'm impressed."

"Knew you would be," he quipped.

Sandy Lynn played along in spite of catching a glimpse of his face and realizing he was struggling, too, although why was a mystery. Their current situation bothered her, of course, so it likely upset him, too, but that wasn't her fault. She had not asked him to stick with her. *Had she?*

Considering everything that had happened in the last day and a half, never mind their distant past, Clay was probably having second thoughts. She certainly was. It seemed as if each event built upon the previous ones until she and Clay had no hope of escaping their forced proximity. At least not in one piece.

After filling her mug halfway, she circled the breakfast bar and perched on a high stool. "I'd have made coffee with these little bottles of water if you'd had coffee and a pot."

"Water's fine." Clay leaned against the counter instead of joining her at the bar and blew on the top of his own mug. "At least my stove worked."

"The trick was finding a saucepan," Sandy Lynn said, grinning. "I found a stainless steel one subbing as a saucer to catch drips from a flowerpot and scoured it out before using it."

"That's comforting." A wry smile was poorly hidden behind the rim of his mug.

"I thought you'd appreciate it."

Movement outside the window over the sink caught

her attention, and she jerked so hard she splashed drops of soup.

Clay was at her side in an instant, his firearm in hand. "What is it? What's wrong?"

"Outside. I thought I saw someone."

"Stay away from the windows. I'll go check."

Sandy Lynn wanted to grab him. To insist he stay with her. She didn't do either; she merely froze where she sat and watched Clay don his boots, then began praying for his safety as well as her own, as he left the condo.

Outside, someone shouted.

Sandy Lynn slid from the stool, crawled beneath the breakfast bar and held her breath, listening to the ensuing silence.

THIRTEEN

Following man-size prints in the snow, Clay had rounded the building. Both hands gripped the pistol, aiming at the sky. The last thing he needed was an accidental discharge of his weapon.

Even though Chief Wright hadn't passed judgment on him so far, an unauthorized shooting wouldn't do much to substantiate innocence. That thought was so ironic Clay almost snorted aloud. Talk about irony. The one cop who was willing to step up and protect Sandy wasn't a cop at all. Not anymore. Meaning he had no real authority, either. Yes, he bluffed well. No, it didn't always work as perfectly as it had on Harper and All-good back at the hospital.

As Clay completed his circle of the condo complex he came face-to-face with Abe Matthews. The cop was in civilian clothes.

Abe waved. "I got your car. Parked it just up the street so it wouldn't tip anybody off that you were home."

"Thanks." Breathing a sigh, Clay holstered his gun. "Why didn't you come to the door?"

"I was about to."

"I mean before. Did you decide to peek in a window to make sure it was me?"

"What?" The thinner man shrugged his shoulders and frowned. "I didn't look in any windows."

Clay palmed the pistol grip, ready to draw again. "You're serious?"

"Serious as they come. Why? Did you see a prowler?"

"Sandy Lynn thought she did."

"How about you?"

"Whoever it was had ducked before I turned around," Clay told his friend. "I did find footprints in the snow. That's why I figured it was you."

"Nope. Sorry. Did you follow them?"

"Yeah. Right back here to where they started," Clay told him. "The street and drive are too icy to register fresh impressions so this is a dead end."

"Okay. Well, if you'll run me back to the station so I don't have to hitchhike, I'll get out of your hair."

"I'm not leaving Sandy Lynn here alone."

"So, bring her. I don't care as long as I don't get in trouble for being AWOL."

Gesturing toward the stained-glass-framed entrance, Clay said, "Okay. Come in for a second while I explain to her. We're having soup. You're welcome to join us."

Abe laughed. "Not unless it's followed by a juicy hamburger and fries."

"Don't I wish. We were too frozen to even think of food before we got here and warmed up a little." When he noticed his friend's raised brows, he felt he should explain further. "Nothing happened, okay? Three bikers chased us all over the back roads, and then we managed to lose them. There was no way either of us could have lasted much longer without a break and dry clothes."

Abe eyed him, head to foot, and drawled, "Ooo-kay."

"Stop with the innuendos. We're old friends, that's all. I didn't even notice that she's a woman."

That brought gales of laughter. Clay was adamant. "I didn't. She's the same lost kid she always was. I feel sorry for her. She's got nobody."

"What about that escaped prisoner? He obviously cares."

"Not for the right reasons," Clay countered abruptly. The two entered the condo together. "Sandy Lynn?" he called.

"Over here." She crawled out of her hiding place with a smile and flushed cheeks. "I was just checking for dust bunnies."

"Right. Find any?"

"Nope. Floor's clean. You pass inspection."

"Good to know." She had begun clearing off the sink and rinsing dishes so he stopped her. "Leave that. We need to talk."

Her gaze darted to Abe. "Did you catch Charles?"

"No. Sorry." A few strides carried him to the open fireplace, where he warmed his open hands.

"Then what?"

The sense that she was again concentrating on him was strong, and Clay had proof as soon as their eyes met. "Abe brought my car. We need to give him a lift back to the station."

"No more sliding sideways on slush and landing in puddles? Hooray."

The other cop scowled at Clay. "What's she mean?"

"It's a long story," Clay alibied. "Let's just say we didn't get iced up by sensible city riding."

"Unbelievable."

Breaking into a grin as he recalled Sandy Lynn's expertise, Clay agreed. "You've got that right. You should see her handle my bike. She's more than capable. She's great."

"Uh-huh. In that case, how did you wreck and get wet?"

Red cheeked, Sandy Lynn didn't reveal their accident so Clay did. "I happened to be driving then, if you must know. She took over when I knocked myself silly."

"Now that sounds like a good story to tell at parties," Abe said, chuckling. "I'm looking forward to hearing all the details."

"Later, maybe," Clay countered. "Right now we need to get on the road so you aren't missed." He locked eyes with Sandy Lynn again. "Go get all your stuff and bring it with you."

"Why? We're coming back here, aren't we?"

Did he dare open up to her about his fears? "I want to be ready for any eventuality, okay? You never know."

A roll of her eyes was her only reply as she left him. That was enough to tell how exasperated she was getting. Well, so was he. It seemed as though their every move was countered too quickly, too perfectly, to be a coincidence. Somehow, Hood and his cohorts were being fed information. They had to be.

Which meant what? Clay asked himself. Was there a link to the insider theft he'd been trying to prove? If so, what was the point of involving Sandy Lynn? There was no way that Charles Hood could be behind the losses from confiscated property.

The connection was Clay, himself, he decided, clenching his jaw. Whoever was out to discredit him had latched on to the attack at the apartment and was using those criminals to wreak havoc on Sandy Lynn and therefore on him, too. So, suppose he distanced himself? Would that help, or was it too late to convince anybody that he didn't care, starting with himself?

One look at her and he knew he couldn't abandon her. Not again. Not now. Not while her life and well-being were still in danger. If he did back off and something happened to harm her, he'd never forgive himself.

Stop thinking of yourself, his conscience warned. *Do what's best for her.*

That conclusion was so logical it was irrefutable. So, what was best? A stint in witness protection would help, of course, but since she wasn't actually a vital witness in an upcoming court case he doubted she fit the criteria. Shipping her out of town, alone, might be a good idea except that would mean she'd be unguarded again, and once her roommate was released from the hospital, that woman would also need a safe place to stay.

Maybe he was thinking too far ahead, Clay reasoned. Borrowing trouble that might never appear. And speaking of appearing, Sandy Lynn was back with the pillowcase luggage. Her damp clothes were draped over her forearm.

"I'll take my jeans, too," Clay said. "They feel almost dry."

"We should have thrown everything in your dryer," Sandy Lynn said. "Wait till those jeans cool off—they'll feel plenty wet."

"They'll dry more in the car," he insisted. "Grab your jacket and boots, and let's hit the road."

"Bad choice of words," she teased with a twinkle in her eye. "Last time we tried that it hurt."

"Very funny."

"I thought so," Abe said, chuckling. "I wish I'd been there to see it."

Clay arched a brow. "Oh? Well, it's a good thing you

weren't or I might wonder how Hood and his cronies found out I had a bike."

The closed expression on the cop's face did not reflect the innocence that Clay had expected. Not even a little bit.

The men relegated Sandy Lynn to the rear seat in the cushy sedan. This was the kind of luxury car she recalled Clay's parents always driving, which reminded her how far apart their relative worlds were. She was the daughter of an alcoholic father and a druggie mom. Talk about opposites! No wonder Clay hadn't taken her teenage confession of love seriously. They'd have made a horrible match.

Running her hand over the leather seat, she marveled at its soft smoothness. It was wrong to covet, she knew, but gave herself permission to at least appreciate riding in such a nice car. Conversation between Clay and Abe caught her attention enough to pull her into the present and hold her there.

Clay was driving. "I'll drop you at the corner so nobody spots us together, if you don't mind a short walk."

"No problem. I'm dressed for it better than you are."

"It's been a rough day," Clay replied. "Did you get me the money?"

"Yeah. As much as I could scrape up on short notice. And a couple of cheap phones. What do you need this stuff for?"

"To keep from using credit cards."

"You worry me, buddy. You're beginning to sound like a guy planning on running from the cops."

"If I have to run it won't be from the law. It'll be for her sake."

A quick tilt of Clay's head to the side indicated the

rear seat, and Sandy Lynn felt the heaviness of a shared concern. So, that was why he'd insisted they bring all the clothing with them.

I should split from him, she reasoned. *That's only fair. But where can I go? What can I do on my own? At least we have wheels again, and who knows when my car will be released or if it's even drivable?*

Her hands were clasped in her lap, her fingers growing icy inside the damp gloves. She was stuck with Clay and he felt stuck with her. Period.

"So there you have it," she muttered.

Clay caught her eye in the rearview mirror. "Have what?"

"A big honkin' mess," Sandy Lynn drawled, letting the sarcasm she felt color her speech.

"Well put." She couldn't believe he was smiling.

"Yeah, well, I do hang out with kids, so I'm bound to pick up their language usage."

"True."

She could tell they were nearing the police station. Clay slowed and pulled parallel to the curb before asking Abe if they were close enough to suit him.

"Works for me, buddy," the taller man said. Once he was out of the car, he leaned in the open door to offer advice. "Keep your eyes open and remember to duck."

"I'll do my best."

Sandy Lynn tapped Clay on the shoulder. "Wait a sec while I change seats. I feel like a reenactment of that movie, *Driving Miss…*"

"Miss Sandy Lynn." Clay patted the empty passenger seat. "My pleasure. Come on up."

Although she followed through with her request, she was already having second thoughts. Why did it bother her so much to sit next to him? It shouldn't. He was just the driver and she merely his passenger. There was nothing wrong with that, was there? No. Of course not.

Nevertheless, she could feel her cheeks warming, so she purposely averted her gaze and stared out the window while she fastened the seat belt. There were plenty of people gathered in small groups on the sidewalk on both sides of the street, and she guessed they were waiting for either court or the release of former prisoners since the jail was located in the same city block, right next door to the police station.

Her eyes scanned the crowd casually, barely registering anyone special, until they settled on a long-haired man in a short biker jacket. It looked like he was talking to a couple of cops. She gasped. Grabbed the door handle with her right hand and reached out to Clay with her left. "Stop!"

Thankfully, all he did was slow their merge into passing traffic. "What's wrong?"

"I saw a biker back there."

"So? They're not all bad, you know. Some are vets and some ride to raise money for charities. They do a lot of good."

"I know, but…that one looked familiar."

"He isn't your ex, is he?"

"No, but he may be an old friend of his. It's been a long time. Still, there was something about the man that definitely made me think of Charles."

"Okay, we'll cruise around the block so you can get a better look."

"Really? Do you think that's a good idea?"

"We'll be safe enough in this car, but you may be right. If he is connected to Hood and sees you in this car, we'll lose our advantage."

Sandy Lynn wasn't about to admit that her thought processes hadn't gotten that far yet. "Let's just go."

"Good plan." Clay threaded the sedan into the slow-moving traffic while Sandy Lynn swiveled to watch behind them.

Her breath caught. She couldn't see the biker anymore, but she did spot a couple of familiar motorcycles parked in tandem at the curb. One was painted exactly the way she remembered Charles's bike. It even had a slightly skewed taillight.

"You're pretty sure, aren't you?"

All she could do was nod and keep watching as the scene faded into the distance.

Clay palmed one of the new cell phones.

"Who are you calling?"

"Abe. If that guy is an escaped prisoner, he can have him arrested."

Sandy Lynn kept straining to see until she lost the ability to pick out details. Feeling anxious and a bit queasy from riding backward, she settled into the passenger seat to look at Clay and listen to his report.

"Abe, listen," he began.

As she watched, she saw disbelief, followed by anger and a touch of fright. "You can't be serious… Well, why didn't you check?"

Apparently Abe had given an excuse that didn't suit Clay because he ended the call and handed her the phone.

"Take the batteries and SIM card out of this one, too. We're ditching it."

"Why? They're only after me, right?"

"Wrong." The muscles in his jaw were knotting, his forehead furrowed and his hands fisted on the steering wheel so tightly his knuckles whitened. "My enemies fixed it so that I'm a wanted man."

"How?"

"Somebody falsified the release papers for this car and Abe fell for it. He walked right into their trap when he brought it to me."

"So, take it back and explain."

"I can't."

"Of course you can. Just turn around and do it."

"With your enemies standing right across the street? No way." Turning a corner so fast she was thrown against her seat belt, Clay floored the gas.

"Maybe it's not them. Maybe I was imagining things. You can't let anybody think you were behind stealing back this car, even if it is your own."

"Don't argue."

"Me? You're the one being irrational. They can't charge you with a crime if you make it right."

"Who says?" Clay kept shaking his head as if he was trying to see a way out. For both of them. Finally he added, "Think. What will happen to you if I get arrested and I'm not here to protect you?"

Although she desperately wanted to deny needing him, needing anyone, the words stuck in her throat. She did need help. His help. Because, like it or not, there was nobody else she trusted as much as she did Clay Danforth. And that included her coworkers and every single other friend she had with the exception of Enid Bloom. Poor Enid. It was Sandy Lynn's fault she had been hurt. That wasn't going to happen again if she could help it, so it stood to reason that she needed to stick close to Clay and ride this one out to the end.

She just hoped the *end* was going to be a temporary condition and not anyone's final breath.

FOURTEEN

Clay entered the Kansas Expressway with his speedometer hovering just over the speed limit, enough to keep them moving fast yet not enough to attract the attention of a zealous trooper. "Did you get the phone apart?"

"Yes." She displayed the interior pieces. "What do you want me to do with these?"

"Toss them. No. Wait. Give them to me."

It wasn't his plan to involve an innocent party, but he saw no harm in dropping the parts of the dismantled cell phone into the back seat of a patrol car if they saw one. Chances of that were slim; however, the idea stuck with him long enough to make him smile.

"What's so funny? I have an odd sense of humor and I don't see any joke."

"I was just thinking about putting those pieces into a police car. Not that we want to get that close, of course."

"Too risky," Sandy shot back.

He sobered. "Yeah, you're right. I'll settle for a dumpster. Keep an eye out for one."

"You'll do better looking in the service area behind some strip mall," Sandy Lynn said.

"In a few more miles. I want plenty of distance between us and the station. Once they issue the order to be on the lookout for us, we'll have to switch to back streets. I want to make the most of this faster route."

"Sensible. So, what are we going to do for communications? My phone is long gone and yours is now toast."

"We'll keep using the burners Abe gave me. And pick up a few more, plus warm clothes, just in case." He reached into his pocket and pulled out a wad of bills. "Count this so we know our limits. We can't stop at ATMs or we'll tip off our position."

"This whole operation is impossible. You realize that, don't you? We can't run forever. And once they catch you, you'll be in much worse trouble than if you'd stopped when I told you to."

"I won't take a chance on losing you." It would not have surprised him to have her snap back at him about leaving her when she was in foster care. Thankfully, she didn't. At least not out loud.

"I wish we could stop and pick up Enid," Sandy Lynn said.

"That would complicate matters even more. We'd have to look after her when we already have our hands full taking care of ourselves."

"Speak for yourself, mister. I'm doing fine."

"Sure, except for the knife-wielding thugs who put your bestie in the hospital and keep chasing you down." Watching out of the corner of his eye, he noticed her smile fade and saw her start to slump against the seat.

"Yeah, there is that. What I don't get is how they know where I am. I mean, once we'd disabled my phone they should have been clueless, yet they kept turning up."

"Or somebody did. Just because a guy rides a heavy

bike, that doesn't mean he's on the wrong side of the law. Some of my friends up in KC ride all the time."

"Can you call on some of them for help?"

"They're cops, Sandy, so, no. Now that the locals are looking for me I don't dare involve old friends. They'd have to choose between helping me and doing their job. They took an oath."

"So did you, right?"

"Yes. And I haven't broken any laws. It may look bad for me, but I promise I'm not guilty of anything except being naive. When I first suspected there was theft going on in the station I confided in the wrong people—or Abe did. Or both."

"You trust him?"

"With my life," Clay said firmly.

"What about with my life?" she asked.

A quick glance told him she was not joking. "I don't trust anybody other than myself to protect you. I'd have thought that would be clear to everybody by now."

"Maybe it is. Maybe that's what's really going on."

He understood what she was trying to say, and part of his mind agreed with her. The best way to undermine anybody was to attack someone dear to them and divert their attention. In his mind he knew that as well as he knew his own name. His heart, however, was far from ready to accept the premise. Backing off from Sandy Lynn at this juncture was too risky. Too foolish.

Though she didn't elaborate, he had to admit she could be right. They had a lot of details to sort out before he turned himself in, including whether or not those bikers were actually working with Charles Hood. Once the escaped criminal was recaptured and interrogated, Clay could make plans to surrender—as long as Sandy Lynn was truly out of danger.

Swinging onto the interstate, Clay merged with the flow of traffic and felt his nerves begin to settle. They'd be much harder to spot amid the evening rush out of town, and now that the sun had set they'd have all night relatively free of worry.

One thing he did think would help was a broader knowledge of his enemy, so he asked, "Why don't you tell me more about your ex? His habits? His quirks? Anything that pops into your mind."

An expression of anguish flashed across her face and was gone so rapidly Clay wondered if he'd imagined it. Then she began to speak, and he knew his eyes hadn't deceived him.

"I hate him."

"And?"

"That's all there is to say. I thought my life before I met Charles was full of problems and disappointments, but I hadn't seen anything until I married him. It was the biggest mistake I ever made or ever hope to make."

Sighing, Clay nodded at her. "I get that. It's not what I'm asking. Tell me about his hobbies, favorite foods, sports teams he followed, that kind of thing. The more I know about him, the better our chances of winning this war."

"That's what it is, isn't it? A war. And poor Enid is a casualty in somebody else's fight."

"If he truly is the one who hurt her, yes. I'm hoping Abe gets the lab results on that spot of blood I found in the closet soon. If it can't be matched to Hood's DNA profile, we'll know you imagined him."

"I didn't imagine anything. It was Charles. I'd know that voice anywhere. I heard it often enough."

"Memories can sometimes fool us. It has been years."

"No. I'm positive it was him at the apartment. I can't

be sure about the bikers because I didn't hear them speak."

"His voice is that distinctive?"

"It is when he's lost his temper and is raging because he didn't get his way. He likes to inflict pain. You can tell it by looking into his eyes when he's got you cornered." She shivered.

"I'm so sorry he hurt you."

When Sandy Lynn looked over at him, there were unshed tears in her eyes and her lips trembled. "You have no idea."

I will not cry. I will not cry, she kept telling herself as the agony of her failed marriage bubbled up in her memory. She had thought, at the time, that she'd loved Charles, perhaps not as much as she'd loved Clay but enough.

"I shouldn't have mentioned him. I am sorry," Clay said.

"Um, no. No. It's all right. I—I just realized how badly I behaved toward him."

"No woman forces a man to hit her. That is what he did, isn't it?"

"Yes, but…"

"No buts. Beating up on a woman is unforgivable. He made that choice alone, not because of anything you did."

But… She knew in her head what he'd done to her was wrong. Physical violence against anyone, other than in self-defense, was inexcusable. Her heart wouldn't let go, though, of how she'd wronged her husband by marrying while she was still in love with someone else. Someone sitting beside her at this very moment. She struggled with this mightily and had to constantly remind herself she'd done nothing to provoke Charles. Nothing. She was the victim. Charles was the perpetrator. Maybe if she thought it enough, she'd accept it. She knew other abuse victims who were facing similar struggles and accepting that they were not responsible for their abuse.

Taking a deep, settling breath, she tried to explain without revealing anything too personal. "I know it wasn't fair to marry anybody, especially not as a means to leave foster care. My foster parents were good people. They did their best. But at that time I couldn't see anything except that I was desperately lonely. Running off with Charles was my way of coping. He obviously came to the conclusion that I'd used him. He lashed out. I may never forgive him for the pain he caused me." She stopped before revealing the termination of her brief pregnancy and the loss of the ability to bear more children. Tears misted her vision.

"I had no idea you were so miserable there," Clay said. "Do you know why I felt I had to leave?"

"No." Shaking her head, she dashed away sparse tears.

"My father was insisting I go to the college he'd chosen and major in business management. I couldn't think of anything more boring. After all, I was just eighteen. The picture of myself, dressed in a three-piece suit and stuck behind a desk all day made me panic. By joining the air force, I was able to break away and take the time to decide what I wanted to do with my life."

"You should have told me."

Looking rueful, Clay nodded. "Yeah. There are a lot of things I should and shouldn't have done."

"It's okay." Sandy Lynn sighed noisily. "We both made enough mistakes for a lifetime."

"You turned out okay," Clay told her tenderly. "Being a teacher is a great profession. Judging by the way you talk about your students, you love them all."

"Almost all," she said, smiling a little. "There are a few who seem unreachable in spite of all my efforts. I can only hope my influence carries through as they mature. Some cases are very sad."

"Like your own, you mean?"

"Yes. Not all come from broken homes, though. Take Charles, for instance. He grew up with both parents always fighting, and in his case that led to his later inability to return love. I can see that, now. A lot depends upon the child as well as their circumstances."

"Are you getting soft on him?"

Sandy Lynn's head snapped around and she swiveled her upper torso to follow. "Of course not. He did terrible things. He—"

"Easy, honey," Clay said. "You don't have to tell me. I can have Abe look up Hood's record and the transcripts of his trial if I need to know more."

With a lump in her throat and her pulse pounding in her temples, Sandy Lynn reached out, clasping his arm. "No. Please. Don't do that. Promise me you won't."

"Why not? Nothing will ever make me think badly of you."

It was so much more than that, and she could barely breathe. If he checked her testimony in Charles's trial he'd know about losing the baby, about the prognosis she'd never be able to bear more children.

A strange calm settled over her. Maybe that was for the best. Perhaps the Lord was answering her prayers for the strength to avoid romance by seeing to it that Clay knew how unsuitable she was for him. Not that God was limited to only one approach, of course. If He wanted to keep her away from Clay there were plenty of other ways to do it.

Finally regaining control of her emotions, she said, "Whatever. It doesn't matter." That was almost true. If she once came to the place where she was able to stop loving Clay Danforth her declaration would become fully factual. Until that time, however, she knew it was vital to keep her innermost feelings to herself.

She'd blurted out words of love long ago and been rebuffed. She was *not* going to make that mistake again.

Their route led to Route 65. Clay took it, heading south, then east. It mattered less where he took Sandy Lynn than it did to simply keep going. The farther away from Springfield, the better, up to a point.

Traveling at night was the most sensible choice, he reasoned. A description of his car must already be out to local and state law enforcement, and they'd have his license plate number, too. Everything was harder to see after dark, giving Clay and Sandy Lynn a temporary advantage.

Clay yawned. Yes, he was weary. And, no, he wasn't going to stop to rest. One quick glance told him that Sandy Lynn had dozed off leaning against the locked door. As long as her seat belt was fastened she'd be safe enough.

Miles roared by. Springfield was far behind them. Before daybreak, Clay knew he'd have to locate a secure place to hide the car, which pretty much excluded motels and hotels along any of the interstates. A B and B might work, providing it was far enough off the beaten path. And small. It had to be so small they were either the only patrons, or two out of no more than four or five.

The fewer people who saw them, the less their chances of being reported.

Driving while Sandy Lynn slept gave him thinking time, and he began to wonder if he'd been wrong about the origin of those bikers. They were just too accomplished, too good at tracking. When she'd asked how Hood would know where she was, she'd triggered a response in Clay's brain that refused to be dismissed.

"How did they know?" he muttered, tapping his fingers on the steering wheel in a rhythmic cadence as a seasonal tune ran through his mind and purred in his throat.

Sandy Lynn stirred. "Um. Tell me you're not humming 'Jingle Bells.'"

"Sorry." Clay smiled over at her. "Want to sing along?"

"Not in a million years," she drawled.

"It is almost Christmas Eve, you know."

"Don't remind me."

He chuckled softly. "It's a little hard to avoid with every town we pass blinking in colored lights."

"Yeah." She straightened and stretched. "Where are we, anyway?"

"My GPS runs off a cell phone so I'm not sure. Somewhere southeast of where we started."

"Do you want me to take over driving so you can sleep?"

"Not unless we can't find a place to stay. I was thinking a bed-and-breakfast. Someplace off the beaten path. Maybe in a small town?"

"Well, we can't go knocking on doors before dawn or they're liable to call the police."

"Always sensible. You're right. I think I'll turn off

at the next opportunity and start traveling back roads. We're bound to find opportunities that way."

"Well, maybe. Don't be surprised if we don't."

"Cynic."

"Realist. The economy has been pretty rough on small businesses lately. I imagine a lot of them have closed."

"Then we'll open them up again," Clay insisted.

"You don't trust me to drive your car?"

"I do. We just don't have time for me to teach you defensive driving and I'd rather be behind the wheel if somebody spots us." As he'd intended, that sobered her.

"You still think we'll be a target? Even this far away?"

There was just one fair way to answer her and he took it. "It's only a matter of time."

FIFTEEN

Sandy Lynn yawned and made a face at him as they passed a brightly lit truck stop with a café. "Coffee. I need coffee more than anything."

"You need a decent breakfast. Both of us do. We have to keep up our strength."

Cynicism tinged her thoughts and her reply. "Sure. We'll be the healthiest victims in history."

"Stop talking like that," Clay said with emotion.

"You're right. I wasn't thinking. I either trust God or I don't. I can't have it both ways."

He was wheeling into the truck stop lot. "No, but you can become disillusioned. Any of us can. It's human nature. And you have been through a lot in less than two days."

"Is that all it's been?" She was flabbergasted. "It seems like weeks, if not months."

"Or just the blink of an eye," Clay countered. "When I look at you it's as if no time has passed at all since we were kids."

"Dumb kids," Sandy Lynn said with a smile. "At least I was. I think you were mostly clueless."

"No argument there." After parking, he circled the

silver sedan and opened her door. "The place smells okay from out here."

"Okay." Pushing past him, she led the way to the double glass doors of the entry. "If it's half as good as it smells I may eat myself silly."

"You can stand it," Clay said, following her in. "My mom is still fighting with her weight, especially since retirement. They moved into a gated community in Florida and seem to love it there."

"I'd wondered. I did mean to ask before I got so distracted." She led the way to an empty booth and slid in, turned over the waiting coffee mug and laid a paper napkin in her lap. A waitress was quick to fill the mug and hand them menus before bustling off with the steaming glass pot.

As Sandy Lynn added sugar and cream, Clay continued. "Your old foster parents moved away, too. I'm not sure where they went, but my mom probably knows. I can ask her."

"Don't." A chill shot along Sandy Lynn's spine and made the tiny hairs on her arms stand up.

"Why not? They were pretty torn up when you ran off. I'm sure it would do them good to learn how well you're doing now."

A lopsided smile accompanied a lift of her eyebrows. "Oh, yeah? Shall we start with the news that my ex is trying to kill me or save that for later?"

"I didn't mean right away. This fiasco won't last forever, you know. The authorities will nab Hood. And now that he's escaped he won't be eligible for parole as soon as he would have been before."

"There is that, yes." Sighing deeply, she sagged against the back of the booth and felt the knot of a wayward spring poke her in the ribs through the vinyl covering.

By using both hands she was able to sip her hot coffee without letting any telltale tremors show. On the outside, she was putting on a performance for Clay to convince him that she wasn't scared. Inside, the butterflies in her stomach were clog dancing like the performers at the Ozark Folk Center, when they weren't trying to flutter up into her throat or pirouetting in circles around her heart.

Pondering her emotional upheaval, she quickly concluded that only a portion of the symptoms were due to the threats on her life. A lot of her uneasiness, her sense of loss, was because of being thrust into close proximity to the man seated across the table. The handsome, gentle, sweet, intelligent, caring...

"Oh, stop it," she muttered to herself.

"Stop what?" Clearly she had captured Clay's full attention when she had not intended to.

Sandy Lynn pressed her lips tightly together and scowled at him. "Stop being so nice, okay? I'd rather you were mad at me."

He laughed behind his raised mug. "I'll try to be sterner from now on."

"Not funny."

"Oh, I think it is."

"Well, I don't. I didn't mean to say anything out loud in the first place."

"Why do you wish I was mad at you?"

How to answer that? She wasn't sure that the plain truth was best. Neither was a lie, of course, so she chose the portion of her answer that seemed to make the most sense. Deciding how to phrase it was another hard choice.

"I don't deserve kindness," she finally said softly, speaking for only his ears.

"Why not? Because you made a few little mistakes in the past?"

"*Big* mistakes," she countered, thinking of her unborn child and mourning all over again. Try as she might to attain forgiveness, her conscience always insisted she was partly to blame.

"Nothing is too big for God," Clay said tenderly. "If you really have renewed your faith, you should know that."

"I don't doubt that He has forgiven me," Sandy Lynn confessed. "I just can't forgive myself."

Instead of laughing at her the way she'd thought he would, he reached across and laid a hand over hers. His touch was warm, the comfort genuine, a sense of peace palpable. "When you hold a grudge against anyone the Lord has forgiven, you're elevating yourself to a position higher than His. Are you sure you're that wise? That powerful?"

"It's not the same thing. You don't know what happened."

"I don't have to." Clay's hands now cradled both of hers. "I believe that Jesus took all our sins on Himself, once and for all. To me, that means that whatever you did, He forgives you as soon as you ask. There are no degrees of guilt, no grades like you give your students. It's pass or fail. In or out."

Don't you dare cry, she ordered herself. *Just don't.* But it was useless. Not only did tears pool behind her lashes, they soon tipped over the edge. Rivulets began to glisten on her chapped cheeks.

Before she realized what was happening, Clay had joined her on her side of the booth and opened his arms. That display of full acceptance loosed a flood that Sandy Lynn could not have stemmed if her life had depended upon it. Somebody cared enough to stay with her, to offer comfort without condemnation. If he knew the whole truth, would he feel the same?

Taking shaky breaths, she managed to pull herself together long enough to reveal her darkest secret. "I—I was pregnant when Charles beat me that last time. I lost the baby."

"Oh, honey, I'm so sorry."

"It was my fault."

"How could it be? You were attacked."

"But—but, I wasn't a good wife. I made him mad. I was always making him mad, making him lose his temper."

Keeping one arm around her shoulders, Clay handed her a spare napkin and waited while she wiped her face and blew her nose. "Is that what happened in your home when you were little? Is that why you thought wives were responsible?"

"They are. I was. I should have protected my baby." Once again, tears welled.

"No, Sandy, you're wrong. Every person is responsible for his or her own choices. The only mistake you made was choosing Hood for a husband. What he did to you later is all on him." He shook his head. "A lot of abuse victims blame themselves. But you're not to blame. You didn't do anything to justify violence. He could have made a dozen different choices if he didn't like what you did or said. A dozen different choices, and not one of them would have involved laying a hand on you."

Searching her mind for a rebuttal, she blotted at the streams of new tears.

Their waitress approached with her order pad and pen poised to write. Thankfully, she paid no attention to the poignant scene being acted out in the booth. "Ready to order?"

"We'll take a number seven and a number three, everything well done, and two large coffees, all to go, please."

As soon as they were alone again, Sandy Lynn sniffled and looked to Clay. "What did you order?"

The smile he gave her was sweet enough to melt her heart. "I have no idea. I just remembered those numbers and didn't want to waste time looking everything up again."

She mirrored his expression. Sniffled. Straightened her spine and nodded. "Well done. And I don't just mean the eggs."

Their order was delivered to the booth in a white plastic bag holding foam containers. Clay stood to leave a tip, picked up their food and paid at the register while he waited for Sandy Lynn to return from freshening up.

The truck stop diner was getting busier as the sun began to peek over the horizon. A couple of tough-looking guys pushed through the doors together, blocking Clay's view long enough for other vehicles to pass. Next, came a black-and-white patrol car.

Clay fidgeted. He'd parked his car around the back, so as long as the cops didn't circle the diner he figured they could still get away. Providing Sandy Lynn hurried.

He stepped back out of the way of the swinging door, looking for different ways out. There was an interior exit that led into the service station part of the building. If he could head Sandy Lynn off and direct her that way, they might have a chance.

He hooked the loops of the plastic bag over one wrist and dug in his pocket for change as he pulled a baseball cap off a nearby display and shoved it onto his head. Using the brim to shade his eyes, he lowered his head to hide his face and tossed the money on the counter for the clerk. What he wanted to do was leave the change, but he figured that might draw attention as he waited for her to complete the transaction and hand over the receipt. "Thanks."

She didn't even look at him. The closed-circuit cameras would have captured his and Sandy Lynn's images, of course, but as long as the authorities didn't know where to begin looking they'd remain anonymous. Stir up any kind of a fuss, however, and there would be no doubt they'd been there.

Clay sauntered past the drink coolers along the back wall and stationed himself close to the door where he expected to encounter her. It swung open. Her eyes were still red and a bit puffy above the smile she gave him when she saw he was waiting. "Sorry to take so long."

Clay cupped her elbow. "Not a problem. C'mon."

There was noticeable hesitation in her response, so he gave her arm a nudge and leaned closer. "A couple of cops just came in. If our enemies have put out a state-wide BOLO they may have our descriptions."

"That's why the hat?"

"Yes. Pull up your jacket hood and don't look around."

Thankfully, she followed orders, also keeping her head down, eyes focused on the path through to the service station section. It took her two steps for every one of his to keep up so he forced himself to slow his pace. "That's it. Easy does it. We don't want to look different than everybody else."

"We are, you know."

"Yeah, I know. The trick is to blend in."

"Okay. You can let go of my arm. I'm blending," she said wryly. "There's no need to hustle me through like a prisoner."

"Don't even think that way," Clay ordered. "You haven't committed any crimes. You're the victim."

"So are you, if you really think about it. We're both innocent."

"And up the proverbial creek at the moment," Clay added. "Just keep walking. We'll go out this door and head for the car. If you see the police car or either of the officers, don't break stride. We don't want them to notice us."

"Gotcha."

He cast her a sidelong glance and marveled at her cool demeanor as they rounded the last corner between them and his car. Even to his trained eye, she looked innocent and unconcerned. "You're very good at this. I wouldn't dream you were trying to be sneaky."

"It's a learned trait," Sandy Lynn replied. "When I was a kid I had to pretend there was nothing wrong when teachers or neighbors asked about my parents." She sighed. "And after I was married, I had to pretend I wasn't scared witless."

"Like now?"

To Clay's surprise she shook her head beneath the hood. "No. I'm not really that frightened now."

"Because we're getting away?"

"No," Sandy Lynn said quietly. "Because you're with me."

For a split second she wished she hadn't been so candid. The gentle smile that lit Clay's face changed her mind. There was nothing wrong with telling him she appreciated his help. Of course not. After all, they were old friends, and as current events were proving, they did need each other. It seemed, at times like the present, he was as happy to be with her as she was to be near him. Those instances might be fleeting, but they were plenty special and memorable.

Sweet memories were all she'd have when this was over, she reminded herself, accepting facts as she saw them. That was okay. It had to be. Every choice had consequences whether a person felt forgiven or not. Just because Clay had insisted that God had erased her mistakes and still loved her didn't mean her problems with her ex would vanish. Ever.

Clay thrust the bag of food at her and clicked his key to unlock the car. "Get in slowly. Easy does it. We need to look nonchalant."

"I know, I know. I won't forget."

"Sorry."

She set the bag on the console between them to free her hands for her seat belt, fastened that, and then pulled the containers into her lap so they wouldn't spill if he ended up speeding again. "All set. What now?"

"Now, we cruise on out of here as if we have all the time in the world."

"Maybe we do." Sandy Lynn peeked out of her hood as they drove past a line of parked cars and trucks. "I don't see anybody around the black-and-white. They were probably just hungry, like us."

"Speaking of which," Clay said, "I'll swing through the next little town we come to and find a place to park and eat."

"Okay. I hope it's soon. It sure smells good."

"I guess it must. I can hear your stomach growling."

"Like a bear coming out of hibernation," Sandy Lynn added, chuckling. In seconds, she'd pulled out the coffee cups and put them into the car's built-in holders, then opened one of the breakfast containers. The aroma was too appealing to ignore. "Yum."

A slice of crisp bacon was calling her name. Manners caused her to first offer it to Clay. "Open up."

"I can't eat. I'm driving."

"Excuses, excuses. I can see passing up pancakes and syrup, but this is finger food." When he failed to reach for it, she held it closer to his mouth.

The glance he shot her as he bit into the first decent food they'd had since yesterday was unreadable. Feeding him had seemed the polite thing to do when she'd begun. Now, however, it was starting to feel too intimate.

As he nibbled closer to her fingers, she released the final scrap. Before she could reach for another strip of bacon, Clay had clasped her wrist and held her hand still. Her first thought was that he intended to lick her fingers, which was far too personal to allow. Nevertheless, she didn't fight him.

"Thank you," he whispered over the purr of the engine. And then he lightly kissed her fingertips.

SIXTEEN

The empty parking lot of a closed tourist center up ahead seemed ideal. Clay pulled in, drove through the entire lot to check for other exits, then parked beside an overgrown bush.

"Okay. Now I can eat." He smiled at her. "If you haven't scarfed it all up."

"We may be a tad short of bacon, but the rest is still here."

Accepting the container she offered him, he opened it. "Forks?"

"And napkins," Sandy Lynn said, providing both. "Can we relax now?"

"For a while. I kept watch behind us. We weren't followed."

"Oh, good. Want some of my scrambled eggs? There's way too much here for me."

"Sure." Holding out his open tray he let her scoop in eggs. "Pancakes?"

"You eat sticky stuff in this beautiful car?"

"It's washable. And speaking of washing, I need to shave unless I decide to grow a beard as a disguise."

Although he hadn't been fishing for compliments, it

pleased him to hear her say, "I kind of like the scruffy look. It's very popular in the movies and on TV."

"Or for criminals who want to change their appearance."

"Speaking of criminals, can you check with Abe today and see if they've caught Charles yet. I still think going back to Springfield and explaining that you weren't running away is the best move."

"I'm not risking your life again."

"I know, I know."

A look of disgust had replaced her smile. That bothered Clay enough to loosen his tongue. "Look. I get it. You don't want me to keep hanging around."

"I never said that."

"You didn't have to. I can see it all over your face."

She said, "That's not emotion, that's breakfast." The quip did nothing to lighten his mood. He knew exactly what was wrong, how she felt, and it was killing him to stick around for more. Truth to tell, it was possible he could drop her somewhere and she'd be okay, but there was no guarantee one or more of their enemies would leave her alone once they were apart. His probably would. Her ex, not so much. Not if he was so bent on revenge that he was willing to stab a woman he mistook for Sandy Lynn.

It didn't take him long to satisfy his hunger. "Hand me what you don't want and I'll dispose of the trash."

She bagged up the remnants and passed them to him with a groan. "I ate too much. I feel like I could sleep for a week now."

"Thanksgiving dinner syndrome. Overeating can make you sleepy." Hesitating at the open car door, he asked, "Will you be okay if I find a place to stay and it's decorated for Christmas?"

"I'll make do with any place that has a comfy bed."

Clay anticipated her blush as soon as she realized what she'd said. He wasn't disappointed. "For sleep. In separate rooms."

"Of course." The embarrassed reaction was almost funny enough to make him smile again. Almost, not quite. It was in the best interests of his heart to keep his mind on reality. Sandy Lynn might be weary, but she wasn't so tired that she'd shelve her morals. For that matter, neither would he. For him, love and respect went hand in hand. The last thing he'd ever purposely do was hurt her in any way.

Driving through the next small town they came to, he found narrow streets, raised sidewalks and closed shops. A tiny restaurant advertised catfish specialties. On a whim, he turned up a side street. One or two more tries and he'd have to give up finding shelter and head on down the road.

Then, there it was. A Victorian-style house, white with blue trim, bedecked in thousands of tiny twinkling lights and red ribbons highlighting shocks of pine greenery. Even the fancy B and B sign in the yard sported Christmas lights and brightly colored round ornaments in clusters at each corner.

Best of all, interior lights shone from several downstairs rooms. Clay tapped Sandy Lynn's arm to get her attention. "Over there. What do you think?"

"Perfect, if they have somewhere we can stash your car out of sight."

"I'll turn around and cruise by more slowly. See what you can see."

She leaned forward to get a good look. "I doubt we'll find a better hideout."

"Having second thoughts?" he asked, worried about

her seeming lack of enthusiasm. "We can keep driving if that's what you want."

She shook her head, never looking directly at him. "No. You must be exhausted. I know I am. If we don't get some sleep we won't be as ready for the next attack."

"It might not come," Clay said, hoping to help her cope and speaking to himself at the same time.

"It will. We both know it will. After we're rested, I want to talk everything over with you."

"Convince me to go back, you mean."

"Maybe, unless you can talk me into staying on the run. I know we needed to get away and work things out. I just think there has to be a better way. Don't you trust anybody in law enforcement anymore?"

"Of course I do. I'm just not sure who. I apparently made mistakes when I first suspected theft."

"Who did you tell?"

The list was short. "My chief and one sergeant. Whoever they told is likely how the word spread."

"And your friend? Matthews?"

"Abe? He'd never cause me grief. Remember how long we've known each other."

"Suppose he thought you were imagining things when you mentioned it? Might he have laughed it off until he saw the problems you were having?"

That notion stuck in Clay's throat like a knot. Was it possible? There was one sure way to tell. If he phoned Abe privately with news of their hiding place and they were subsequently accosted he'd know for sure. Doing that before they'd had a chance to sleep and recover, however, was foolish. Perhaps tomorrow, he reasoned. Or the next day, although that was Christmas Eve, providing he hadn't totally lost track of time.

Lights in front of the Victorian illuminated the shady

covered porch area. A single bulb burned above the back door. Clay parked in the most secluded spot and escorted Sandy Lynn to the rear door.

A polite knock brought a wiry middle-aged woman who was wiping her hands on a white butcher's apron. "Morning. You folks lost?"

"No," Clay replied with a smile. "We made the mistake of thinking we could drive all night and now both of us are beat. Do you have any rooms available? We'll need two."

"Two, huh. You been fightin'?"

He chuckled and went along with the woman's error. "Nope. I'm afraid I snore like a freight train."

"Me, too, son," she said, grinning. "C'mon in. I'm about to take a pan of biscuits out of the oven and the coffee's made."

"Thanks." Standing back, he urged Sandy Lynn in before him. "Coffee will be nice. We ate about half an hour ago or we'd gladly take you up on the offer of food. So, you do have vacancies for us?"

"Got one now and will have another by ten or so," she said. "I need to spiff up the second room and change the linen after the current tenants check out."

"That's a relief. Can we wait in here? It's cold outside."

"Thought we might have fresh snow for Christmas, you know, add to the ambience," the woman said as he held a kitchen chair for Sandy Lynn and then joined her. "Where y'all from? Is there snow over your way?"

"A dusting," Clay said before changing the subject. "Those biscuits smell wonderful. Wish I was hungry."

"All home cooking here," she said proudly. "Too bad so many travelers pass us up on the holidays."

Sandy Lynn finally found her voice. "Really? That's

a surprise. I mean, you've decorated so beautifully it's a shame more people won't see it."

It surprised Clay to hear her praising the Christmas theme. "It is pretty," he agreed. "You don't have bookings for tomorrow or the next day?"

"Nobody but the two of you. Guess you're the answer to my prayers." She set two mugs of steaming coffee on the table for them.

"How so?"

"Don't pay attention to me. I tend to get a bit broody this time of year. Miss my husband, don't you know."

"I'm sorry," Sandy Lynn said.

Clay was reluctant to ask if the older woman's husband had passed away. Turned out he didn't need to.

"Killed in the line of duty, he was. Right around this time of year, too. There were a couple of years I had to force myself to keep going and save this business all by myself."

Line of duty? There was little doubt what that meant. He clenched his jaw. If they up and left now, they'd raise all kinds of questions in the woman's mind, questions he'd rather not have to answer. Worse, she might decide to get in touch with some of her late husband's cronies and bring them into the situation.

He stood. "Tell you what. Why don't we let my— wife—have the available room right away. I'll wait down here, maybe in the parlor if there's room, until your current guests check out."

"Suits me." She pointed a gnarled finger. "Stop off at the front desk and fill out a registration card, will you, while I finish cooking. The only key hangin' on a peg out there will be yours. It has the room number on it. I'd go with you, but I don't want to burn this food."

"No problem," Clay said, "Mrs....?"

"Proctor," she said, "Everybody calls me Bessie."

"Thank you, Bessie." He pulled out Sandy Lynn's chair, having to practically lift her to her feet to make her move. With one arm around her waist, he shepherded her to the foyer and located the described desk. Not only did the front of the house smell like pine and gingerbread, it was filled with memorabilia and charming Victoriana.

Sandy Lynn was hesitant. "What are you going to write on the card?"

"Nothing, for the moment," Clay replied. "If she remembers to ask again I'll think of something. In the meantime, I want you to take this key—" he unhooked it "—and go on up to the empty room. I'll look after things down here."

"Bessie said…"

"I know what she said. Sounds like her husband was a cop. That won't make any difference."

"What if she takes after him? Married couples sometimes adopt each other's habits. Suppose she gets too curious?"

"One dilemma at a time, please," Clay said. "You go on up and lock the door after you. I'll knock when I've brought in our luggage."

"Luggage? You think she won't wonder why we packed in pillowcases?"

That almost made him laugh. "It beats plastic grocery bags. Don't worry. I'll sneak them in while she's busy with breakfast. Now get into your room before anybody else sees you."

Halfway up the carpeted staircase, Sandy Lynn paused and looked down at him. "I forgot all about Enid. We promised to take clothes to her. I should call and tell her I was delayed."

"I'll take care of everything." He pointed forcefully. "Go!"

Once she had disappeared at the top of the stairs he blew out the breath he'd been holding. A cop's widow. Of all places to stop, they had to come here. At times like these Clay couldn't help wondering if God was for them or against them. Concluding it could be both, he shoved his hands into his pockets and sauntered back toward the warm kitchen, intending to conduct an impromptu interview with Bessie Proctor. They had to know if she was still closely connected with law enforcement or if the loss of her husband had turned her against his profession.

The answer to that question would probably determine how long he and Sandy Lynn stayed, and whether or not he dared close his eyes and rest for even a few hours.

Hair on the back of Clay's neck prickled. "I'm going to run out and get our stuff from the car," he told the landlady.

She never turned from the stove as she called, "Glad to have you here. Merry Christmas."

After having been uprooted and stuck in a car half the night, Sandy Lynn was more than ready to kick back. Admittedly, the bedroom suite was lovely, not too fussy, not too plain, and done in a restful blue-and-aqua color scheme that complemented the light gray tiles in the adjoining bath. That was the only part of the accommodations that wasn't from the Victorian era and, even then, the sink stood on a footed pedestal the way a pitcher and bowl would have in the old days. Under other circumstances she would have loved to stay there for weeks.

Thin walls were the only drawback. She listened to the couple in the adjoining room talk while packing to leave. They sounded so happy, looking forward to seeing family again and attending a big holiday gathering. Sandy Lynn had never seen the appeal of that kind of party. Her idea of bliss was a carton of mint chip ice cream, a spoon and a fire in the fireplace. Her former apartment had lacked a real hearth, but the one at Clay's condo had been nice to sit in front of, even without the ice cream.

Thoughts of him brought back the manic butterfly feeling in her stomach and made her wish she didn't have such a vivid imagination—she was beginning to find it easy to picture him in her life. To stay.

An image of him as the father of the big family he'd always said he wanted made her daydream fade. Clay would make a wonderful dad someday. She just wasn't cut out to play the part of the mother of his children. Not now. Not ever.

Sandy Lynn kicked off her boots and stretched out on top of the coverlet. How did a person like her escape the imprints of such a harrowing childhood? Would she have been as poor a mother as her own was? That notion cut to the heart until she realized she truly did love her students.

Meaning to shower and change as soon as she had the opportunity, she allowed herself a moment's repose, eyes shut, and was awakened by a sharp rapping on her door.

"Open up. It's me," Clay called.

Momentarily disoriented, she stood and went to let him in. Instead of a calm entrance, he burst through and slammed the door behind him.

Half-asleep, she rubbed her eyes. "What's gotten into you?"

"I was downstairs talking to Bessie, and she happened to mention that she's throwing a party for her husband's old unit."

That was a waker-upper. "What? When?"

"Tomorrow. I'd like to stay here and rest, and I'm sure you would, too, but we don't dare."

Sandy Lynn eyed the comfortable bed where she'd been napping. "Not even for one night?"

"No. We need to get a head start. I'll pay her for two days and we'll pretend we're staying."

"But we won't?"

"No, we won't. Tonight, after she's turned in and the house is quiet, we'll sneak out and hit the road again. In the meantime, you can nap. I'll keep watch."

"We'll share the watch," Sandy Lynn countered. "I'll sleep first and as soon as you get access to your room, come and tell me so I can stand lookout from my window. I can't imagine anybody will locate us, though, can you?"

"Not logically. If we hadn't been tracked before I'd be positive."

"And you're not, even now?"

"No." Clay was shaking his head and raking his fingers through his hair. "Sleep in your clothes so you're ready to leave immediately."

"You really expect me to go to sleep again, after you showed up wired like this? Give me a break." She glanced at the comfortable bed. "Tell you what. I'll go downstairs to talk to our landlady and you can grab a few winks while I'm gone."

"No way." He was adamant.

"Yes, way. The more time that passes, the greater

our chance of your car being spotted. It's safer for me now than it would be later. Plus, sometimes women will share info they wouldn't tell a man."

"Like what?"

She wanted to shake him, to shout. Instead, she shrugged and smiled. "If I knew that I wouldn't have to ask, would I? I'll see if she has any more plans for Christmas that will cause us grief." She pointed to the bed. "In the meantime, crash. That's an order."

"Oh, yeah?"

Sandy Lynn stood her ground, hands fisted on her hips, her jutting chin and steady gaze proving her stubbornness. "Yeah."

Clay's shoulders began to sag. He yawned and stepped aside to give her access to the door. "Well, okay then." A smile lit his weary yet mischievous expression.

Realizing she had won this skirmish, Sandy Lynn returned his smile. "Glad you've finally come to your senses."

When he countered with, "I don't have any sense left," she chuckled under her breath.

Descending the stairs, she pondered past events. In retrospect, neither of them had behaved rationally after that first encounter when he'd helped save Enid's life. The only good thing was that her bestie had survived.

Well, that and the fact that Clay was sticking around. Before entering the kitchen, she paused in the foyer for a quick prayer of thanksgiving. No matter what his motives might be, she needed him.

"Thank you, Father," she whispered, her heart opening despite misgivings. "Thank you for sending Clay back into my life." As a postscript she added, "Please look after him, too," and meant every word.

SEVENTEEN

Bessie was nowhere to be found when Sandy Lynn reentered the kitchen. Amiable-sounding conversation was coming from an adjoining dining room and she followed the sounds. Four other guests, probably two couples, were enjoying a sumptuous breakfast.

She acknowledged them with a tiny wave. "Sorry to bother you. I was looking for Mrs. Proctor."

The closest guest gestured with his fork. "Kitchen."

His companion, a woman with flaming red hair and enough eye makeup to stock a cosmetic counter, disagreed. "No. Remember, honey? She said she was going outside for a license number or something."

"That's right," the second woman agreed.

Sandy Lynn could barely speak. "License number?"

"Yeah. Something about a missing registration card." The red-haired woman waved a manicured hand in dismissal. "Probably just a paperwork glitch. She is running this place all by herself, you know. Want to eat with us?"

"Thanks, no," Sandy Lynn managed to squeak out. "I should go find Bessie." Which she was definitely *not* going to do. Not before telling Clay what she'd just learned. If Mrs. Proctor was jotting down the license number of his car she'd be in a position to ID them once she tumbled to the fact that they were wanted by the police. Given her husband's background, the woman was more than likely to pass that information on to law enforcement. Then they would know where Clay had gone and could concentrate their search.

Feeling as though there were wings on her feet, she ran up the stairs. The door to her room was locked and Clay had the key so she knocked. Hard. Repetitively.

His eyes were narrowed, his jaw set, when he jerked open the door. "Quiet."

Sandy Lynn pushed past him and whirled. "We have to leave. Now."

"Why? What's happened? Did you see bikers?"

"No. Not that. It's about the registration card we didn't fill out. Bessie, Mrs. Proctor, was outside writing down your car license."

"How do you know?"

"The other guests told me."

"Are they sure?"

She waved her arms in the air. "Who cares? If it isn't happening right now, it will soon. Leave her money on the bed if you want and let's get out of here."

"You're right," Clay said, sounding disappointed.

"It's not my fault."

"I know, I know." While he was donning his boots, he pointed to the top of the old-fashioned dresser. "Check out that tourist info and see if there's any place listed that looks promising. There's probably a map in there, too."

"A map? We have GPS on the second new phone, don't we?"

Clay nodded briskly. "I don't plan to use that any

more than I have to, okay? Not even to contact my attorney. Just grab those brochures and let's go."

Though it was hard to keep from being short-tempered with him when he was issuing orders, Sandy Lynn held back. This situation with Charles was hard on her, yes, but it was imperative that she remember she and Clay were both being adversely affected. Could his problems be tied to hers in some way? Try as she might, she couldn't imagine how.

He grabbed the pillowcases and eased open the door before handing their belongings to her. "I'll go down first, in case there's trouble. When I signal you, head for whichever door is unwatched and go wait in the car." He handed over his keys. "Lock yourself in, just in case."

"I've heard that before."

A shrug. A scowl. "Completely different circumstances," he said aside, his voice rumbling enough to give her the shivers.

Together, they started for the narrow stairway. A faint voice drifted up to them. A woman's voice.

Clay halted and held up his hand. They paused, almost to the ground floor, and listened.

"That's right," the voice was saying. "I didn't write it down when I heard it on my scanner, but I'm pretty sure it matches. You'd best get somebody out here. On the double." A pause. "Okay, bye."

Sandy Lynn didn't know the numbers and letters of Clay's license plate. She didn't have to. The tension in his body told her enough without words.

He reached back for her hand and clasped it tightly. "That changes everything. We're done sneaking. Stay with me. We're going to march out of here as if we have every right to."

The idea that they didn't have that right hit her like

a sledgehammer. For the first time since they'd fled Springfield she realized they were no longer merely misunderstood, innocent parties to crime. They were actually wanted fugitives!

Turning themselves in seemed sensible. So did staying on the run. With no current information on Hood or the men trying to put Clay in jail, surrendering might be the worst option.

Nevertheless, her conscience insisted they must do the right thing. Sandy Lynn bit her lip. If she knew what that *was*, she'd be delighted to comply.

Still holding her hand, Clay paused at the foot of the stairs, braced for battle if necessary. Conversation in the dining room provided a hum of undertones. No one was currently speaking loud enough for him to overhear. Therefore, he figured Bessie had concluded her phone call and was probably briefing the other guests.

A shadow moved in the kitchen, then vanished. If the landlady was replenishing the breakfast coffee, they might have a chance to get out the rear door without being observed.

Tiptoeing to the doorway and seeing no one, he waved behind him for Sandy Lynn to proceed. She slipped past silently and swiftly, and was almost to the rear exit when he heard a stir coming from the dining room.

Bessie appeared. She wasn't alone. Two youngish men stood at her sides. To Clay's relief, nobody looked armed.

"Stop," the older woman demanded.

"No. Run for the car," Clay told Sandy Lynn.

Concentrating on the other three, he laid his palm

on the grip of the pistol tucked into his belt. "We don't want any trouble. We just want to leave."

"What's she got in the bags?" Bessie's voice was shrill.

"Our stuff. We haven't stolen anything. I left money for our room on the bed upstairs. You won't be out anything. Just don't try to stop us."

The owner of the B and B held out her arms to block the other guests. "No need for violence. I've had enough of that in my life already. Just go if that's what you want. Get out of here."

Resignation in the woman's expression caused Clay to reply, "Thank you," before following Sandy Lynn.

She was not only in the car, she'd started it. He tossed the pillowcases into the rear and jumped into the passenger seat. "Okay. Let's go. Show me what you can do."

"Seriously?" Her exuberance in spite of their harrowing situation almost made him laugh.

"Yes. Get us out of here."

Applying enough power to proceed without skidding, she backed out, shifted and started toward the highway. He supposed he should compliment her on her driving because she deserved it, but he didn't want to make her complacent. This was merely the beginning of another stage in their toxic adventure and, judging by recent experience, it would worsen before it was over.

They stopped at a red traffic light at the edge of town and Sandy Lynn looked over at him. "Where to? Which way?"

"Beats me."

"I had a chance to glance at a map in a brochure while I was warming up the car. The Mark Twain forest isn't far. How about heading in that direction?"

"Suits me. Do you know the area?" he asked, surprised when she said she did.

"There's a summer camp nearby. I went there six months before I was sent to the foster home next door to you," Sandy Lynn explained. "Maybe I can find it again. It's not marked on that map, but I know it was close to an abandoned ranger station because we used to sneak off and hide there to smoke." She made a face at him. "My wild youth. I haven't smoked since."

"Good for you."

"Thanks."

Clay kept watch behind them as they moved farther and farther from civilization. The brown-and-green sign designating an entry road into the forest was up ahead. "There."

"I see it. This still okay with you?"

"Fine. I'd feel better if we had camping equipment, though."

Sighing and smiling slightly, she glanced over at him. "Picky, picky, picky."

"Nag." Clay felt the beginnings of a grin.

When she responded, "Cynic," he couldn't keep from smiling, so he bent over the simple map and traced parts of it with his finger as a mental diversion. "I think we can cut through and exit on the opposite side if we want. It's an option."

Sandy Lynn nodded. She'd slowed their speed due to the winding, narrower road. "Good. All we'll have to do is choose between facing Charles and his biker buddies, running from the police or freezing to death because we didn't come properly equipped. That sounds like a perfect plan."

If her conclusions hadn't been so spot on, Clay would have laughed aloud. Instead, he clamped his jaw and studied the map for other choices, discovering none. Maybe entering the forest hadn't been such a bright idea after all.

It looked to him as if, should they be discovered too soon, they were likely to be trapped there.

Relying on instinct as much as memory, Sandy Lynn steered along a series of back roads and dirt tracks that took them in and out of deeply wooded areas. Pines predominated, although it was evident that beetle infestations in the past had decimated certain sections.

"Finding the camp would be a lot easier if everything had stayed the same," she offered.

"You're lost?"

"No. I'm merely exploring various probabilities."

"Do you expect any of these roads to lead to the camp, or do you just enjoy driving my car?"

"I'd like it a lot more if we'd stopped for gas before we came up here," she said with a grimace. "We're down to half a tank."

"I get good mileage. Don't sweat the small stuff."

"Humph. Yeah, and it's all small stuff, right? Isn't that what you used to say?"

"Not anymore," Clay said with a quiet sigh. "I'd welcome that size problem right now."

"Ditto."

After passing two possible turns, she spotted a worn, faded wooden sign nailed to a tree. The arrow aimed right. She braked and pointed. "Can you read that?"

"No, but there's a picture of a tent."

"Good enough for me."

The next few miles flew by at the speed of a freezing lizard in January, and Sandy Lynn was becoming discouraged. Her spirits took a further dive when the camp came into view and she saw its dilapidated condition. "Not the way I remember it."

"Is it even the same place?"

"Beats me." She stopped in front of what looked like it had been the main lodge building. "Maybe we can find something to eat in here if the mice and squirrels haven't beaten us to it."

"Don't hold your breath. I could use a couple of Bessie's hot biscuits about now," Clay said.

"You could thank me."

Clay made a silly face at her as he got out. "For...?"

"For my exemplary driving and perfect sense of direction."

He stepped up on the porch and she was sure he was chuckling before he said, "Watch yourself. These boards look rotten."

"Kind of like my idea to come here," she added with a grimace.

"I've heard worse." Clay was grinning. "Matter of fact, I've *had* worse. Recently."

"I wasn't going to mention it."

"Thanks." He held out a hand to her, and she grasped it so he could help her navigate the rickety porch.

"At least we'll have plenty of wood if we decide to build a warming fire."

Clay chuckled low. "You can't burn the porch, okay?"

Sandy Lynn laughed and pointed with her free hand. "I meant that stack over there."

"Oh. Okay. C'mon. Let's explore."

It didn't take long for her to decide it was going to be rough housekeeping there, not to mention sleeping. The fact that they located some canned goods that were within their best-by date seemed amazing when she thought about it. "I've never eaten cold beans before."

"It helps if you're really hungry. That ham stuff in the square cans stays good for years after its sell-by date."

"I'll take your word for it." She'd located a linen closet and brought out a blanket that had been stored in a sealed bin. Throwing it over what was left of a sofa made sitting there a little less undesirable. It did not, however, make her feel comfortable about the prospect of sleeping later.

Clay lit a fire in the fireplace and soon had the room tolerably warm. A long stick made a satisfactory skewer and allowed Sandy Lynn to hold a chunk of faux ham over the fire until juices dripped and it almost caught fire.

She rescued her meal and burned her fingers. "Ooh! Ow! Hot."

"Ya think?"

"I hope it's worth the pain. It's been a long time since breakfast."

Clay opened his mouth—she assumed to answer her—then froze and raised one hand. "Shush."

"What?" The look on his face quieted her far more than his warning.

Then she heard it. A vehicle was approaching, low gear grinding as it climbed a hill. Since their approach had seemed less of an incline, she assumed somebody must be approaching from a different direction.

"We never should have lit this fire. Somebody must have seen the smoke from the chimney."

"It was a calculated risk. My decision, I'm sorry to say," Clay told her.

"Now what? Hide? Run? Face them?"

"First we see who it is," Clay said. "Try to look innocent and clueless, will you?"

"Innocent is natural. The clueless part will be harder."

"Well, try. And stay out of sight unless I call you. I'm going to go greet our visitor."

Dropping the skewer and jumping to her feet, she started after him, her arms reaching, the urge to grab and stop him stronger than any hunger pangs. "No. Don't go. Don't leave me."

The poignancy in her own voice and the sorrowful look in his eyes transported her straight back to her teens and made her wonder if Clay was experiencing the same sense of déjà vu.

"Please," she added, then stopped halfway across the room and watched him close the door behind him, cutting her off. He had to come back, to be okay. He just had to. She didn't think she could bear it if something awful happened to him.

The sound of a pleasantly called greeting did little to ease her tortured mind or slow the pounding of her heart. Peeking out through grimy glass in a window was no comfort, either. The vehicle idling in front of the building, putting out clouds of exhaust and fogging the icy air, was a green pickup with the Forest Service logo on the door.

Though the ranger wasn't technically a cop, he was still an arm of the law, meaning he had the power to arrest them.

She saw Clay shake the man's hand and watched him gesturing as he apparently explained how they had ended up in an abandoned building.

The ranger once again offered to shake hands. Clay accepted, then turned while the other man sauntered back to his truck. Sandy Lynn's ragged breathing echoed in the silent room, accompanied by occasional popping sounds from the dying fire.

After entering, Clay eased the door closed behind him. "I told him we'd gotten lost and were too tired to drive safely so we took refuge here. I think he bought it. I promised to make sure the fire was completely out before we left."

Since she had remained at the window, it was easy to see the green truck. Exhaust clouds had ceased. The engine was off. With a grab for Clay's arm, she drew him closer and tilted her head to point.

"I don't think he was fooled," she said, feeling dejected. "Look. He's not going anywhere."

Clay's eyes narrowed, his brow furrowing. "And while he's parked out there, neither are we."

EIGHTEEN

Clay couldn't decide who he was most angry with, finally settling on himself. That conclusion brought other choices he'd been putting off making, one of which was phoning Abe for assistance and thus revealing his position. He hated to involve his best and perhaps only real friend; in this instance, however, there didn't seem to be a lot of options, and those he did have weren't good.

Zipping up his leather jacket, he stepped out onto the back porch for privacy. One advantage he had was knowing Abe's private cell number, which was a lot better than having to contact him through the station. When he connected, Clay felt a lot better.

"Matthews."

"It's me. What's happening back there?"

"In Springfield? Beats me. We got a tip from some Podunk police department in northern Arkansas that your car had been spotted. We're on the road, heading your way."

"Bessie," Clay murmured.

"Um, right. The informant was a Mrs. Bessie Proctor. How did she manage to spot you, let alone write your license number down?"

"I'll explain everything as soon as I get Sandy Lynn to safety. I suppose there's been no word on her ex."

"Matter of fact, we thought we were closing in on him when we got orders to abort that assignment and go after you. Chasing a rogue cop ranks higher than some low-life wife beater, although it should be a toss-up if you ask me."

"So, you still don't have Hood in custody?"

"Nope. Last I heard he'd hijacked a patrol car and an Arkansas unit was in pursuit."

Clay's blood iced in his veins and he braced himself against the log exterior of the main cabin. If the escaped convict was or had been in a police car, that meant he could also have been listening to the radio and heard the same dispatch Abe had.

"We may as well have put up a billboard," Clay said cynically. "If everybody doesn't already know where we are, they soon will. There's a forest ranger parked right out front, and judging by the way he's been speaking into his mic he's probably figured out who we are, too."

"Hold on. Radio traffic."

Clay overheard most of the broadcast information. Not only had Clay's car been spotted before they'd entered the forest, the ranger parked out front had just confirmed their location. Things were looking worse by the minute. At this point, all Clay dared hope for was that the good guys would arrive before anyone else showed up.

"How far are you from the Mark Twain forest?" he asked Abe.

"GPS says twenty minutes, give or take. A ranger is guiding us in."

"Terrific."

"Hey, don't blame him. He's just doing his job."

"Who else is with you?" Clay asked, holding his breath for the answer and praying it wasn't one of the cops he suspected.

"Who isn't?" Abe cracked back. "Even Chief Wright went mobile for this call."

"Did he happen to bring Detective Johansen?"

"Yes. Why?"

"Because both of them seemed to believe I'm innocent. Other than those two, and you, I don't place a lot of confidence in fairness."

"Well, nobody can just shoot you to end the investigation if we're watching," Abe said.

"Thanks, buddy," Clay drawled. "That makes me feel a bunch better."

"You're welcome. I'd also count the ranger as a neutral party. That's one more ally."

Clay nodded even though Abe couldn't see him. "Yeah. If Allgood or Harper come up, keep an eye out. I don't trust either of them."

"Will do." Sirens started in the background, almost drowning out the phone call. Abe shouted, "Keep your head down. We're getting close."

Clay ended the call. If this was to be a standoff, he'd have to find a safer place to stash Sandy Lynn to keep her out of the line of fire—providing she'd do as he told her. The woman had a mind of her own, which wasn't so bad if lives weren't at stake, particularly hers.

He ducked back inside, pocketed the phone and found her warming her hands by the fire. The moment she saw him her eyes filled with moisture. "The truck is still out there."

"I figured it would be. Come here."

Her steps were measured, her arms slowly rising as if to embrace him. What could Clay do other than respond in kind? As she leaned on his chest, he completed the hug and pulled her closer. "It's almost over. I promise."

"I told you to never make me another promise."

"This one's different," Clay insisted. "This one can't fail."

"So, we'll be all right? You'll be all right?"

Leaning down to place a featherlight kiss on her hair, he momentarily closed his eyes and imagined another time, another place. He wondered if it would ever be possible to undo his mistakes regarding the extraordinary woman in his arms.

His mind told him, no, while his heart continued to ask and pray and hope for the opposite.

Given the option, Sandy Lynn would have languished in Clay's embrace forever. Since that wasn't possible, she chose to take the initiative and relieve him from bearing her burdens as well as his own.

She gathered her convictions and gently pushed him away. "If I take to the forest and make a lot of noise, maybe the ranger will decide to follow me and you can escape."

"I'm not going anywhere without you."

Relief flooded her. She closed her eyes and took a ragged breath. "I won't argue. So, what is plan B? I know you must have one."

"Only keeping you safe in any way I can."

Her keen mind had been mulling over various scenarios and had settled on what she felt was the most likely to succeed. "Here's what I think we should do. We need to split up." When he opened his mouth, ostensibly to protest, she placed her fingertips on his lips to silence him. "Hear me out."

A slight nod was followed by a kiss on her forehead. "Go on."

"There are lots of other cabins around here. Some are really close by. If I run one way and you go another, the ranger can't follow us both. Then, whoever is free waits for Abe and explains everything."

"We can wait together. There's no reason to split up."

Tell him the rest of your plan, her heart insisted. *Give him logical reasons to listen to you.* If she'd thought for a second Clay would agree with her ideas, she'd have followed the urge to open up to him. Unfortunately, his brain didn't work like hers and she was afraid he'd stubbornly disagree. All she wanted to do was get one of the good guys alone, away from questionable companions, and totally convince him that Clay was innocent.

Success would depend upon her powers of persuasion, as well as the other person's open-mindedness, of course, but by separating, Sandy Lynn envisioned their chances doubling. One of them could reason with the ranger while the other talked to the men in the first police car to arrive. Having officers on the scene would also soothe her worries about Charles Hood and his cronies. She almost hoped they would show up so she and Clay could resolve both their dilemmas at the same time.

Sandy Lynn's pulse thudded in her ears, nearly blocking out incoming sounds. That's why she wasn't sure she was hearing the approach of sirens at first. Apparently, Clay had also heard something different, because he left her and went to the window.

"The ranger just got out of his truck again," he announced. "I'm going to leave my gun in here and go stand with him so there won't be any questions about whether or not I'm surrendering. I don't expect the cops to approach with guns drawn, but I'm not willing to take the chance on one of the crooked ones trying to shoot me."

"Then you should stay in here," she argued.

"No. Out in the open."

"I'll come, too."

"No. You stay in here and wait for me to settle things outside. When I'm positive the right people are in charge, I'll call you out."

"Suppose they just arrest you without giving you a chance to explain? What then? They'll haul me back to Springfield, and Charles will have more opportunities to murder me."

"Concentrate on your faith," Clay countered. "It'll bring you through."

Oh, how she wished that was true. In Sandy Lynn's eyes, faith was best utilized as a part of a sensible lifestyle, not relied upon in place of common sense. God had given her a brain. He expected her to us it, period, not sit back and wait for heavenly intervention when earthly choices could save the day. Or preserve life, for that matter.

Clay opened the front door and called, "I'm coming out," then held his hands away from his sides and stepped onto the porch.

Sandy Lynn had never taken off her jacket in the chilly log building. She'd wait for Clay's signal, as he wanted. If and when he secured a promise of peace and safety for them both, she'd appear. If he did not, she'd do her absolute best to get Abe alone and do whatever he recommended to help Clay.

Pacing didn't help pass the time. Neither did imagining various rescue scenarios that brought her and Clay through unscathed. What she craved almost to the point of tears was action.

There was a rear door off the kitchen that led into the forest. If she took that and circled around, keeping out of sight, she'd be okay. After all, the ranger was parked close by.

All the way into the large commercial kitchen, Sandy Lynn felt a sudden chill in the air, as if a door was open. Or had been. She stood motionless, waiting, looking, listening. No threats were apparent, so why was the hair at the nape of her neck rising? Why did she feel so uneasy all of a sudden?

She tiptoed to the door, planning to ease it open enough to check the surroundings. Stainless steel sinks were uncluttered yet dusty. So was the tiled floor. As she scanned it, choosing her path, she noted a disturbance in the dirt. Footprints. Recent ones with waffle treads. Had Clay ventured that far away from her while looking for food? It was possible.

Raspy breathing and her own heartbeats were all Sandy Lynn could pick out over the wailing of the approaching sirens. If only they would quiet down, she thought, so nervous she was trembling.

She reached for the door handle, her fingers poised above it. There was nothing wrong with her plan, yet some unnamed instinct kept telling her to stop. To reconsider. To do as Clay had ordered.

Suddenly all options were taken from her. A large, gloved hand clamped over her mouth and strong arms pinned her to a man's chest. She could hardly breathe, let alone scream for help, though in her mind she was shrieking.

A harsh voice whispered in her ear. "Stop fighting

me, Sandy, or I'll quiet you down the hard way. You know I can."

No one had to tell her who was restraining her. She didn't have to see her ex's face to feel the power of his hate. Yes, she did know what he was capable of. And it wasn't pretty.

"Don't scream," Charles hissed as he eased the pressure of his hand over her mouth. "I'm warning you."

Sandy Lynn managed a tiny nod and gasped to replenish the air in her lungs as soon as he allowed it. Deep breathing helped clear her head and consolidate her thoughts. If Clay walked into this mess, he was sure to be injured, perhaps killed, because he was unarmed. What could she do? How could she possibly alter the circumstances to give him a fighting chance? For one thing, she had to get Charles and whoever may have come with him to leave this building before Clay came back for her.

"The—" she coughed "—cops are coming. Don't you hear them?"

"Yeah, I know." The escaped felon laughed as if she'd told a joke. "They led me right to you."

"How?" Feeling a slacking of his hold, she twisted away to stare at him.

"Police radio. I borrowed it." He displayed a small, portable unit. "Had to mute it though, or you'd have heard me coming."

"You can't stay here," she offered, hoping Charles would agree and take her farther from Clay for her old friend's sake.

"We aren't," he said with evident sarcasm. He reached for her upper arm.

She let him take hold even though memories of his rough treatment screamed against it. This was for the best. For Clay. And maybe, just maybe, she'd be able to turn the tables on this hateful man and see him brought to justice again. It was worth a try. Worth a wordless prayer. Worth sacrificing herself if that meant Clay and the others would be okay.

Love for her old friend filled her heart and mind, driving out the agony over past disappointments. Peace came in a wave and washed over her, leaving an invisible covering that felt as though she was wrapped in a warm blanket. Cosseted. Protected. Under divine guard.

Charles opened the rear exit and shoved her through the doorway. She stumbled. He kept her from falling, pushing her ahead of him and up the incline into the trees where two more men waited.

"Please, Father God," Sandy Lynn whispered to herself, "stay with me no matter what happens. Please, Lord?"

Gray clouds blocked the sun and the temperature in the forest was bone-chillingly low. Adrenaline kept Sandy Lynn moving, picking her way across rocky, leaf-strewn ground while Charles jerked her arm from time to time, likely to keep her aware she was his prisoner. The other two men took positions on either side, ostensibly to guard their leader, and they started to skirt a small, outlying cabin.

Pieces of loose bark snagged on her jacket. Snow crunched beneath her boots, making a faint squeal as it compressed and she slipped a tiny bit.

Two of the bikers dragged her up to the derelict cabin and shoved her through a narrow door.

"Tie her up and gag her," Hood ordered.

"I won't fight you, I promise," Sandy Lynn told him.

All he did was laugh at her and motion to his companions by waving a gun.

I won't give up. I won't quit, she assured herself as the powerful men bound and gagged her. *I'm not done living.*

That final thought gripped her heart and refused to let go. She wasn't done. Not by any stretch of the imagination. She somehow knew she had a lot time left. Even if she wasn't able to spend it with the man she loved, at least she was saving his life.

I do love Clay, Sandy Lynn admitted ruefully. *I probably never stopped.* Tears spilled down her cheeks. Her breath clouded in the cold air. Movement around her didn't register until she was grabbed roughly and pulled to her feet.

The gag kept her silent as Charles dragged her across the rough cabin floor, opened a closet and shoved her in. Its walls smelled of cedar. There was barely enough room to turn around. Sandy Lynn screeched behind the gag and rued the moment of past weakness when she'd foolishly confided her fears to him.

Charles slammed the door. A lock clicked. Being in the dark and confined to a small space made her shake and hyperventilate until she collapsed from the effects of sheer panic.

Dark. So dark. And musty with the smell of vermin and moldy wood. She felt her knees start to give way and she leaned against a wall. Her tears were rivers. Her forehead beaded with sweat despite the cold.

And all the while her brain kept on screaming. And screaming.

NINETEEN

The arrival of a line of patrol cars, including Arkansas State Troopers, was preceded by an unmarked Missouri sedan. Chief Wright quickly exited, in the company of Detective Jim Johansen, and went straight to the ranger's truck.

Again Clay displayed his empty hands for everyone's benefit because the regular officers that had followed were fanning out, acting as if they considered him a dangerous criminal. He did not intend to give anybody a reason to start shooting.

Apparently, neither did Chief Wright, who waved them back with a firm order. "Stand down."

Harper and Allgood, pausing off to one side, were the last to holster their weapons. Clay concentrated on them for a split second before addressing his chief. "I'm glad you came, sir. Johansen, too. Cooler heads are needed around here." He gave the ranger a nod. "Present company excluded."

"Care to explain what's going on?" Wright asked. "Did you really kidnap a crime victim?"

"What?" That was almost laughable. "Of course not. I'm trying to keep her alive. That's why we ran. Her ex is after her. He'd already knifed Enid Bloom in the apartment they shared."

"It was you who spotted the blood in the doorjamb?"

Clay nodded. "Yes, sir. I was hoping it would be a match for Hood."

Johansen spoke up. "You were right. It was. When I met Ms. Forrester at the hospital she seemed to be friendly with you. I hope you can prove she left town of her own volition."

Clay gestured toward the cabin. Allgood twitched when Clay moved, so he once again raised his hands enough to allay any suspicions he was armed. "I left my gun in the building behind me. Sandy Lynn is in there too, waiting for my signal to come out. She can vouch for me."

"Then I suggest you call her," the chief said. "Let's get to the bottom of this and go home. And while we wait, suppose you tell me why you broke into impound and stole a vehicle."

"Whoa. I didn't steal anything. It's my own car." Clay scowled at Abe. "Matthews showed me a release."

Abe agreed and faced the chief. "The form I was handed looked legit. It was only after Clay was out of town that I found out it was bogus. By that time, he'd already left Springfield and the warrant was issued. I figured we'd be able to set things right as soon as he came home."

Clay was not happy. "You knew I wasn't coming back until Sandy Lynn was safe. Why didn't you tell the chief I didn't steal the car?"

"It didn't matter what I said at that point," Abe alibied, blushing. "You'd already violated his orders by leaving." He looked to the chief. "After Hood stole a patrol car I was sure he'd be nabbed. The danger would be over, and Clay would come back so we could explain everything to you, together."

Grabbing his friend's arm, Clay frowned deeply. "Hood is still on the loose?"

"Afraid so."

Clay stared at the log building, trying to catch a glimpse of Sandy Lynn through the dingy windows. There didn't seem to be any movement inside. "We need to get her out here with us, ASAP. For her own safety."

Wright agreed. He motioned to a nearby police officer. When Clay saw it was Allgood, he stepped into his path and stopped him. "No. Not him. Anybody but him or Harper."

"Out of my way." Allgood kept advancing.

"You'll have to move me."

"That can be arranged." He palmed his holster.

Abe Matthews stepped between Clay and the other officer while the chief intervened verbally. "This has gone far enough. Matthews, give me a reason why you're interfering with my orders. And it had better be good."

"Because he's the guy who gave me the fake release," Abe said. "He and Harper were both involved. I found pieces of their handiwork in the trash by Harper's desk after it was too late. That's how I knew the paperwork wasn't genuine."

"Okay, so we dummied up a release for the car," Allgood said. "It was just a joke. Nothing serious. Danforth had orders to not leave town, with or without his car."

Clay had long suspected that this particular cop was guilty of crimes much worse than printing false paperwork. Arching a brow, he asked, "Chief, did you read the last report I filed on thefts of confiscated property?"

Wright smiled for the first time. "I did, although it

would have helped if you'd named names. Matthews, here, explained what he knew about your prior connections to Ms. Forrester, too. Now, shall we get her and head back home to sort this all out? It's freezing and some of us are out of our jurisdiction."

"Yes, sir. Gladly," Clay said respectfully, in spite of the fact he was now a civilian. Waving an arm, he called, "Sandy Lynn. You can come out now," as he started toward the porch.

Clay climbed the rickety steps and raised his voice. "Sandy?"

The door opened with a squeal of rusty hinges. Clay stepped inside. "Sandy! Come on out. Everything's okay."

Still, there was no reply.

Clay motioned toward the crowd gathered outside. His voice was strong, but his feet felt as heavy as two Mack trucks. "I don't see her. She's not here."

Air inside the cramped closet was barely breathable, yet Sandy Lynn could not stop gasping and began sobbing as soon as she'd worked the gag loose and spit it out. Being this close to panic made her picture herself standing at the edge of a cliff, her toes touching the edge, a yawning abyss beyond. The image made her dizzy, nauseous. Her pulse thudded in her head, in her temples, as if her vessels could barely contain the pressure.

This degree of hysteria had occurred for the first time when she was younger, in her initial foster home, when two of the older girls had thought it would be funny to lock her up and leave her there. By the time her caregivers had found and released her, she was slick with sweat, exhausted from screaming and crying and

smelled of urine. Fear was soon replaced by embarrassment and she'd run away, only to be found and taken to
a different home, and three more after that, until she'd
landed with the couple who'd lived next door to the
Danforths. To Clay. He was the reason she'd stayed.

"Think of him," she told herself in a hoarse whisper.
"Think of Clay, not where you are or who put you here."

Doing that did help some. So did wordless pleas for
deliverance formed as prayers. It didn't matter that none
of her thoughts were that coherent. She knew God heard
her and would sort it out. The problem was waiting.
Keeping her head was hard when she wanted to scream
her throat raw and kick at the closet door until her toes
ached. Not knowing where Charles and his buddies had
gone was secondary. By now there had to be lots of police with the ranger and Clay. That was a plus.

"If I get out of this… No, *when* I get out of this, I'm
going to do whatever it takes to get Clay's chief to understand why he disobeyed orders to stay in Springfield and helped me run away. It's not fair for him to
be blamed. He was only doing the morally right thing,"
she whispered to herself.

Although her raspy breathing continued intermit-
tently she was becoming calm enough to reason. She'd
used her hands to pull the gag loose. Maybe she could
use her teeth to untie the rope. Trying not to think about
who or what had had prior access to the rough, twisted
cords, she curled her lip, sucked up her courage and bit
into the knots. They were gritty. The texture turned her
stomach and she tasted bile on her tongue.

Suddenly the closet door was jerked open and Sandy
Lynn almost tumbled out. Hood caught her. "I might
have known you'd try to get loose," he growled. "Come
on. We're all leaving."

There was little Sandy Lynn could do to deter them except make herself hard to carry, so she pretended to faint, going limp and trusting him to keep her from actually hitting the floor.

Hood cursed. Someone else laughed, taunting him with pointed comments about his choice of women. *Well, fine. Whatever worked*, Sandy Lynn thought. She had to slow him down to give the police time to locate them. What she hadn't anticipated, and should have, was the unleashing of his violent temper.

He hauled her to her feet in front of him. Before she could collapse again the flat of his beefy hand caught her across the cheek and sent her reeling. She bounced off the wall. There was no way she could squelch a screech of pain.

"Faking. That's what I thought," Charles shouted. "Get up and get moving or I'll give you more of the same."

Had the cops overheard? She doubted it. Not inside, with doors and windows closed. But if she was dragged outside, the silent forest would be the perfect backdrop for a blood-curdling scream that would echo off the hills and let everyone know she was in trouble.

She began to cooperate, not so much that he'd think she'd surrendered totally but enough that he might neglect replacing her gag. All she needed was one chance. One unguarded opportunity to let loose a high-pitched howl that would put a frantic wolf to shame.

It would have to be quick, she told herself. And very, very loud, because Charles was sure to react with more physical punishment. She'd felt his wrath often enough in the past to know how much he could hurt her. That didn't matter. She couldn't let herself think of anything except warning Clay and at the same time alerting the police.

It would have to be the best screaming she'd ever done. And she'd have to be braced for retaliation. It was certain to come. Hard, fast and painful.

"God, help me," Sandy Lynn whispered.

Even if it wasn't much of a prayer, it was all she could manage. A simple plea and quiet thankfulness for the faith that she knew would sustain her in the moments ahead.

Clay had reclaimed his pistol on the sly and tucked it into his belt, pulling his jacket over it. He kept searching the empty building, hoping with all his heart that Sandy Lynn was merely hiding. Chief Wright had sent Abe and several other officers, including Arkansas State Troopers, inside to offer assistance. Nobody turned up the missing woman.

Logical progression led him to the rear door where he noticed spots of water on the floor and crouched down to examine them. Melted snow? Had someone's boots carried it in? "Over here," he called to the others. "Back here."

Skirting the small puddles, he gave the door a hard shove. It swung partway open and stuck there. Through that opening Clay could see a uniformed cop climbing the incline toward one of the outlying cabins. *Who? Why?* Had Wright sent him?

"Everybody. Look," Clay shouted, pointing. "Who's that, and what's he doing up there?"

Nobody seemed to know. Since they had all entered the lodge at the same time, a lack of information made sense. "Abe, run back and ask the chief if he sent other uniforms to search the forest," Clay ordered. "The rest of you, follow me."

Clay was well aware he had no authority. Nevertheless, he gave orders as if he were commanding his former security unit in the air force. That sufficed. A couple of the troopers trailed after Abe Matthews while three more stuck with Clay. As long as they didn't try to stop him he was glad for the backup.

The cop above not only reached the small cabin, he ran up onto the porch and was greeted by a door opening to admit him.

"Take cover," Clay said firmly. "Something's off."

Expecting gunfire, he continued climbing by zigzagging from tree to tree, always keeping a solid trunk between himself and the cabin.

Tracks in the snow and mud led straight to the building where he'd spotted the cop. The desire to see a smaller set of prints among the others was so strong it made Clay wonder if he was imagining the imprints of Sandy Lynn's boots.

Just then, a piercing scream echoed off every tree, every rock, every patch of ice and snow, making the hills seem as if their very substance was in agony.

Clay broke cover and ran straight for the cabin, his heart racing, his feet pounding the slippery ground. He faltered once. Twice. He recovered quickly, pushed himself up and went on. Men were shouting behind him.

He raised his gun and worked the slide to chamber a live round.

His guttural cry of "San-dy!" was so emotional it surprised even him.

A lot was happening around Sandy Lynn that she didn't understand. Her ex had dragged her outside, as she'd hoped, and silenced her with a single blow, but that didn't keep her from picking out one special voice among all the others. *Clay!*

The cop who had been so readily accepted by Charles looked familiar. Despite her tension and fear, she knew she'd met him at the hospital in Springfield. What was he doing here in Arkansas? And why wasn't Charles treating him like an enemy?

Head pounding and vision blurred, limbs quaking and weak, Sandy Lynn curled up on the ground, knees to her chest, and tried to recover while she listened.

Charles was laughing. "Good thing I looked before I shot when you showed up," he taunted the officer.

"You'd better watch it," the cop warned. Hearing him speak provided enough info for Sandy Lynn to recall his name, which proved to be an oxymoron, since it was Allgood and he was all bad.

She didn't move. What in the world was going on?

"What do you want," Hood asked with evident rancor.

"That girl. I'm gonna be a hero and rescue her to prove what a great cop I am."

"In a pig's eye."

"Hey, you owe me. I told you where to look, didn't I?"

"Not this last time," Hood snapped. "I found her myself."

From her position on the icy forest floor it was impossible for Sandy Lynn to tell whether the two men were actually aiming directly at each other, but it sure looked as if they were. She knew it was wrong to wish either of them harm but if the choices of who got hurt widened to include Clay, it was no contest in her mind.

Distant voices echoed. The two thugs who had been helping Charles fled. Revving of motorcycles followed. Sandy felt a strong pull on her arm and struggled against it.

"Stand up and come with me or I'll shoot you where you lay," Charles yelled.

Allgood made a grab for her other arm. "No. Give her to me!"

Strung between the two like a rag doll, Sandy Lynn managed to free herself from both and stagger backward.

Allgood also backed up, taking a shooter's stance on the uneven ground with a safe distance between himself and the escaped felon.

That was when she saw Clay round the corner of the cabin. He was alone, although there was enough commotion behind him that she knew more help was close by.

Allgood took his eyes off Hood. Recognition lit his eyes. He whirled to aim at Clay.

Positioned slightly uphill and to Clay's right, Sandy Lynn anticipated what was about to happen and launched herself toward the man she loved, not thinking of herself for an instant.

There was a bang, a flash to her right and a passing blur at almost the same moment.

She landed before her scream died back. A tremendous weight pressed her into the rocky ground. Was this what it felt like to die? There was no pain to speak of, although she was having terrible trouble breathing.

A gentle voice called her name. She tried to rise, to answer, and failed. Other people were there now. Their shuffling and shouting mingled with her own pulse beats. *A pulse!* She still had a pulse! *Praise God,* she was alive.

The weight eased. Someone was lifting Sandy Lynn,

cradling her, talking to her. "Sandy Lynn. Are you hurt?"

It took a couple of deep breaths for her to regain her speech. "I don't know." She glanced at her hands and saw blood. "Am I shot? It doesn't feel bad."

"I don't think so," Clay said, lifting her in his arms and stepping away. Charles lay below, on the ground, unmoving. It was Clay she'd meant to spare so how had her ex become involved? And what had happened to Allgood?

A brief glance answered that question. The rogue cop was being physically restrained by state troopers and was babbling incoherently about self-defense.

She replayed the previous moments in her mind, recalling the blur she'd barely noticed. Had that been Charles? Why?

Tears spilled down her cheeks and she looked up. "Did—did he try to *save* me?"

"Looked like it to me," Clay said, nodding. "We'll never be able to ask him, but I like to think he had a little good in him. Nobody is all bad. Not even the worst of us."

"Unbelievable." It was barely a whisper.

"If he could hear me I'd thank him," Clay told her with tenderness.

Sandy Lynn thought she detected a break in his voice and clung to his neck while he carried her away from the scene of the fatality, all the while raining kisses down on her hair and forehead. It took all her remaining fortitude to battle the urge to lift her face and offer her lips for one last, beautiful experience. But she could not. Not now. Not ever. Everything was over in more ways than one. Charles would never again harm her. And, hopefully, Allgood would confess to framing Clay for theft.

Sadly, her time with Clay was also at an end. He would go back to the life he'd had and she would return to teaching after the holidays. There could be no other ending to their story, to the love that was never meant to be. Without her, he could look forward to building the big, happy family he'd always wanted. With her, that was impossible. Yes, she loved him enough to let him go, and no, it wasn't going to be easy.

All the way back down the hill to the cars she continued to weep tears of regret, of guilt, of thanksgiving, and for the love she knew she must deny. For Clay's sake. Because she loved him so much.

EPILOGUE

Sandy Lynn escorted Enid home in a taxi on Christmas Day. Their landlord had readied the apartment above their prior one and had told Sandy that Clay no longer resided on the ground floor.

Enid's brown eyes widened with glee when she stepped through the door. The tree was magnificently adorned with lights, ornaments and tinsel streamers. There were holly garlands draped over every door, and live poinsettia plants bloomed in decorative pots in the living room, kitchen and dinette. She grabbed Sandy Lynn's hand. "Oh, honey, it's beautiful. You didn't have to go to all this trouble. It must have taken you half the night to put this up."

Sandy Lynn was almost struck dumb. "I—I—I didn't." Her jaw gaped in wonder. "Maybe the landlord decorated when he and his wife moved our belongings."

A man's answer echoed from the hallway leading to the bedrooms. "It was elves. Really big ones."

Enid laughed. Sandy Lynn was too shocked to do anything other than smile, particularly because she wasn't sure she recognized the voice. She did, however, have the presence of mind to help her roommate to the sofa and settle her with care.

Before she had a chance to investigate, Abe Matthews popped around the corner into full view. He was wearing a green felt elf's hat with bells on it. Sandy Lynn managed a smile for him. "Thank you. It really is lovely. We both appreciate it, don't we, Enid?"

"I'll say." She patted the couch cushion next to her. "Come take a load off, Mr. Elf. You must be worn out doing all this by yourself."

Grinning, he joined her. "I had a little help."

"Oh, you did, did you?" Enid was grinning from ear to ear, her expression less one of surprise and more one of self-satisfaction.

Sandy Lynn rolled her eyes. "All right, where are you, Clay? You know how I feel about putting up decorations. Come on out and take your punishment like a man."

"Who? Me? I'm just an innocent elf." Matching green felt hat in hand instead of perched rakishly on his head the way Abe's was, he emerged from the hallway.

"Innocent? I do understand why you and Abe did it, though, so I'll cope. For Enid's sake."

"Maybe by next year…" Clay began.

Sandy Lynn stopped him. "No. Not next year. As soon as Enid is back to normal, I'm going to move away and find a job in an area that doesn't hold so many bad memories."

"What about the good memories?"

"They all come with dark shadows. It's best if I just leave."

"You don't have to. I'm being reinstated, so you won't have to be ashamed of me."

"I never said I was." She didn't like the intense concentration she was getting from all three of her companions.

"We can start over if you want," Clay offered. "You know. Date. Like normal people. Get to know each other better." He hesitated before taking several steps closer and reaching for her hands. "Don't you believe that God brought us back together? Everybody else does."

Sandy Lynn pulled away, turned her back, bit her lower lip and wondered how she was going to explain her decision in front of witnesses, particularly such interested ones. "I plan to stay single for the rest of my life so you may as well give up."

"I'm never giving up on you, lady. Never. Got that?"

She sensed his approach and felt his light touch on her upper arms. "No! Just no, okay."

"Why?" Clay released her and stepped back. "I told you my legal problems were solved. Allgood confessed as part of a plea bargain and all charges against me were dropped so an association with me won't negatively affect your teaching job."

"It's not that. I still don't understand all the ins and outs of what's been happening. What does that have to do with my ex?" Sandy Lynn asked.

"I admit that had me stumped, too, until I learned that Charles was almost as much a pawn as you were. Allgood fed him information about you in the hopes that my helping you with your problems would keep me too busy to figure out who was framing me."

He paused and smiled. "So, what are you doing for dinner tomorrow night?"

"It's not that simple. You don't understand."

"I will if you explain," Clay said tenderly. "Please?"

From her place on the sofa, Enid broke in. "If you don't explain I'm going to tell him, honey. It's only fair. He's obviously crazy about you."

Sandy Lynn whirled on her friend. "Don't you dare."

As Abe slipped his arm around Enid's shoulders and she leaned into him for moral support, Clay intervened by facing Sandy Lynn and saying, "She doesn't have to spell it out. I read the trial transcripts. I know about the damage Hood caused and I want to spend the rest of my life helping you get over the trauma."

"You want a big family. You always said so. I can never give you that." Tears were coursing down her cheeks.

"Fostering or adopting is a good alternative. You know what it feels like to be an outcast. Think of all the lost kids you and I can help. But I can't do it alone."

"That's not the same," she argued, sensing that her resolve was starting to slip away.

"In some ways it's better," Clay countered, reaching for her hands. "I love you, Sandy Lynn Forrester. I did before, although I was too young and inexperienced to realize it. We've both done things we wish we hadn't, but that's all behind us."

Sniffling, she reached for a tissue, using the time it took to blot her tears to make up her mind, once and for all. "And?"

Clay looked confused. "And what?"

"And we have years to make up. Are you going to ask me to marry you pretty soon or make me wait forever?"

Cheers from the sofa filled the room as Sandy Lynn stepped into Clay's waiting embrace and clung to him.

"Merry Christmas, Sandy Lynn," he whispered into her ear. "Will you marry me?"

"Merry Christmas," she echoed. "Yes."

* * * * *

Dear Reader,

Like Sandy Lynn, I have problems with all the glitz and hoopla surrounding the secular celebration of Christmas. There's nothing wrong with being joyful and spreading good cheer. It's simply the memories of past experiences that tend to dampen my enthusiasm for decorating my house or putting up a Christmas tree these days. If you want to help me celebrate, find one of those Angel Trees and take a child's name to buy gifts for. Or give an extra gift to a charity for children. Kids need to know someone cares about them. We all do. I wish you the most blessed, peaceful Christmas of your life, this year and for all the years to come.

I love hearing from readers, so feel free to email me at val@valeriehansen.com, follow me on Facebook or go to my website at ValerieHansen.com for more info about books and all my goings-on.

Blessings,

Valerie Hansen

COMING NEXT MONTH FROM
Love Inspired Suspense

SEARCH AND DEFEND
K-9 Search and Rescue • by Heather Woodhaven

Undercover and tracking the assassin who killed his partner, FBI special agent Alex Driscoll accidentally pulls his partner's widow, Violet Sharp, and her search-and-rescue K-9, Teddy, into the case. Now, with Violet's life on the line, they have to work together to bring a killer to justice...and stay alive.

ROCKY MOUNTAIN STANDOFF
Justice Seekers • by Laura Scott

Someone will do anything to get federal judge Sidney Logan to throw a trial—even target her six-month-old foster daughter. And it's up to US Deputy Marshal Tanner Wilcox to keep Sidney and little Lilly safe. But with a possible mole in the courthouse, trusting anyone could prove lethal...

WILDERNESS HIDEOUT
Boulder Creek Ranch • by Hope White

Regaining consciousness in the Montana mountains with no memory of how she got there and an assailant after her, Dr. Brianna Wilkes must rely on a stranger for protection. But when hiding Brianna puts rancher Jacob Rush and his little girl in the crosshairs, they have to survive the wilderness *and* a killer.

TEXAS RANCH REFUGE
by Liz Shoaf

After cowboy Mac Dolan and his dog, Barnie, stop an attempted abduction, Mac is surprised to learn the target is Liv Calloway—the woman the FBI contracted him to investigate. Letting Liv hide from her pursuers on his ranch provides Mac the perfect cover. But is she a murderer...or a witness being framed?

COLORADO AMBUSH
by Amity Steffen

A mission to solve the mystery surrounding her sister's suspicious death sends Paige Bennett and her orphaned niece right into the path of ruthless gunmen. And jumping into Deputy Jesse McGrath's boat is the only reason they escape with their lives. But can Jesse help Paige uncover the truth... before it's too late?

BURIED COLD CASE SECRETS
by Sami A. Abrams

Searching for her best friend's remains could help forensic anthropologist Melanie Hutton regain her memories of when they were both kidnapped— and put her right back in the killer's sights. But can Detective Jason Cooper set the past aside to help her solve his sister's murder...and shield Melanie from the same fate?

LISCNM1221

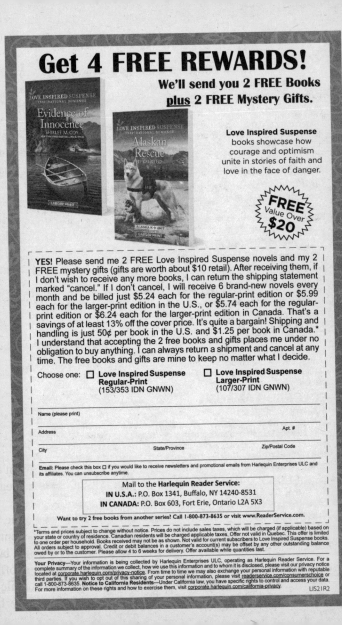

"We're being followed…"

"I'm heading for the police station."

"Finally, something that makes sense." Bracing her left hand on the dash, Sandy Lynn did her best to stay in one place on the seat.

Clay turned corner after corner. "I thought you said…"

A hard smack jolted her car and snapped her head back against the support at the top of the seat.

Survival leaped into her thoughts as she called out wordlessly to her heavenly Father.

The car was hit again. Clay righted it.

A harder smash followed quickly.

Clay hollered, "Hang on!"

They went airborne, diving nose-first into a drainage ditch.

Sandy Lynn saw Clay's head snap forward just as the airbag engulfed him. The passenger side of the dated vehicle was not equipped with crash protection, so the seat belt was the only thing keeping her from flying through the shattering windshield.

Breathless and shocked, she just sat there…wondering if their pursuers were going to stop to finish them off.

Valerie Hansen was thirty when she awoke to the presence of the Lord in her life and turned to Jesus. She now lives in a renovated farmhouse on the breathtakingly beautiful Ozark Plateau of Arkansas and is privileged to share her personal faith by telling the stories of her heart for Love Inspired. Life doesn't get much better than that!

Books by Valerie Hansen

Love Inspired Suspense

Emergency Responders

Fatal Threat
Marked for Revenge
On the Run
Christmas Vendetta

True Blue K-9 Unit: Brooklyn

Tracking a Kidnapper

True Blue K-9 Unit

Trail of Danger

Military K-9 Unit

Bound by Duty
Military K-9 Unit Christmas
"Christmas Escape"

Classified K-9 Unit

Special Agent

Visit the Author Profile page at LoveInspired.com for more titles.